In Shining Armor

KNIGHTS in shining armor,
    Knightly vows and quests,
Valor, dreams, romances
In your waving crests!

IN
SHINING ARMOR
OF
MY BOOK HOUSE

EDITED BY

OLIVE BEAUPRÉ MILLER

PUBLISHERS

THE BOOK HOUSE for CHILDREN

CHICAGO

21

PRINTED IN U.S.A.

CONTENTS

The BUGLE SONG
Alfred Tennyson

The Splendour falls on Castle walls
  And snowy Summits old in Story;
The long light shakes across the lakes,
  And the wild Cataract leaps in glory.
Blow, bugle, blow, set the wild echoes flying,
Blow, bugle, answer, echoes, dying, dying, dying.

DONN P. CRANE

Una and the Red Cross Knight
Retold from Book I of The Faerie Queene
Edmund Spenser

ow Glo-ri-an'a was that greatest, most glorious Queen of Faeryland and she did keep her feast for twelve days every year, nor might she at that time refuse to any man or woman what boon soever he desired. It happened once when that her feast was just begun, there came before her throne a tall young man of clownish mien and rustic garb. He made request that she should give to him the right to ride forth and redress whatever wrong should first at that great feast be brought for justice unto her. The Queen must needs consent, though after that, the youth, full humble in his bearing, withdrew far from her throne and sat him with the rustics who squatted on the floor.

Soon came a lady fair in mourning weeds. She rode a snow-white ass, and with her came a dwarf who led a warlike steed and bore the arms and armor of a knight. The Lady, falling prone before the Queen, made sad complaint how that a fearful dragon kept her father and her mother shut up within a castle whence he suffered them not to issue. Weeping, she besought the Queen to give her some good knight to work deliverance for these twain. That clownish person, then upstarting, desired that he be given this adventure. The Queen much wondered and the Lady much gainsayed; yet did he press his case, full earnest in desire. Then cried the Lady: "This armor which my servant bears will fit no man save one of greatest faith and courage, uprightness and truth. If you it fits I will accept you as my knight."

The armor then was put upon the youth. It fit him perfectly and in it now he seemed the goodliest man in all that company. The Lady Una liked him well. Eftsoons, he took the vows of knighthood and departed by her side, wearing on breast and shield, a blood-red cross in memory of his dying Lord and likewise to declare that he would battle only in the cause of right and truth.

The Lady Una rode upon her snow-white ass, her face well veiled from sight beneath her ample wimple, and over all her garments a trailing long black robe, as one who ever mourned for that old King and Queen, shut up in prison by the dragon. Beside her, on a line, she led a snow-white lamb, as pure and gentle as her heart, and far behind the twain the dwarf with lagging steps bore Una's bag of needments on his bended back.

Now as they passed along, the sky was overcast, and rain came pouring down. They would not face the storm but left the beaten highway and sought shelter in a grove—

> Whose lofty trees, yclad with summer's pride,
> Did spread so broad that heaven's light did hide,
> Not pierceable with power of any star.
> And all within were paths and alleys wide.

Beguiled with bird-songs here they wandered on in peace as though no tempest raged without, but when the storm was done and they would leave the wood, they found no path to lead them. Dark and gloomy were the trees; dense and dismal that black forest. So many paths there were, so many tortuous turnings, that they wandered round and round and ever deeper in. Alas, they two were lost. This was the Wandering Wood, where in a hollow cave, there lurked a monster vile, who breathed forth dark enchantments and hated God and man. By force of her dread spells whoever entered here was soon so sore bewildered that he took the false for true, and so was doomed to wander in a circle hopelessly.

Straight on her darksome cave came Una and her Knight; but Una's eyes were clear to pierce the wiles of falsehood. Not long was she deceived. She knew now where they were.

"Draw back!" she cried. "Draw back!" And sensing all the weird unspoken horror of the place, the dwarf quoth shrilly, "Fly! This is no place for living men!"

But he, the youthful Knight, all fire and hardihood, could not be stayed for aught. Dismounting from his horse, he looked within the cave. His glistening armor made a little glooming light, by which he saw the monster half serpent, loathsome, foul. Forth came the serpent, hissing; but seeing light of armor, she sought to turn and flee, to seek her den of darkness. The Knight leapt on her boldly. He made her face him squarely and do battle in the light. Lifting high his sword, he struck a powerful stroke. She reared herself up fiercely. She wound her tail around him, till hand and foot she bound him. Then Lady Una cried:

> "Now, now, Sir Knight, show what ye be,
> Add faith unto your force and be not faint!"

At sound of her dear voice, the spirit welled within the Knight. He freed one hand and seized the monster by the throat. He forced her to unloose the coils that held him bound. In rage she then spewed out a flood of poison from her mouth and in it frogs and toads, her offspring, loathly, foul. These, swarming all about, climbed up the good Knight's legs and sore encumbered him till with one mighty blow he struck the raging beast and clove her evil head from off her evil body. Coal black, her blood gushed forth, whereon her ugly brood, finding now no more their wonted refuge in her mouth, plunged in that coal black stream and perished one and all.

IN SHINING ARMOR

Fleeing then that spot, the victor and his lady followed steadfast one clear path until it brought them safely outside the Wandering Wood. But now it chanced they met an aged man in long black robes. Sober he seemed, and simple, and ever as he walked he bent his eyes full humbly on the ground, and seemed to pray. The Red Cross Knight saluted him and asked him if he knew of any bold exploit that needed to be done. The old man answered that he lived in quiet far away from wordly cares; yet if these two would rest the night with him, he could upon the morrow lead the Knight unto a wild man's lair. Thus might he soon destroy a brute who ravished all the land. So did the Knight, content, permit the man to lead them home.

> A little, lowly Hermitage it was,
> Down in a dale, hard by a forest's side,
> Far from resort of people that did pass
> In travel to and fro.

In rustic quiet here, the old man entertained his guests with store of pleasing words as fair and smooth as glass. But when came drooping night and lids weighed down with weariness, he led them to their lodgings and bestowed them there to sleep. Then he sought his magic books and threw aside in secret the holy Hermit's guise; for this old man, enwrapped in well appearing words, was Ar-chi-ma'go, a magician, the foe of all things good. He knew upon what quest the Red Cross Knight was bound, and ever fiercely hating to see a good deed done, he was resolved by spells to bring that quest to naught. So long as all true holiness within the good Knight's heart should dwell in closest union with Una's clear-eyed wisdom, they were invincible. Apart they would be powerless. He must separate the two.

With weird and devilish spells he called forth evil sprites that fluttered in the darkness like flies about his head. From these he chose out two, the falsest of the lot, and one he sent to Mor'pheus, the powerful god of sleep, to fetch an evil dream. The other with his charms he made into a lady most like to lovely Una. Coming where the Knight lay peacefully in slumber, the evil sprite from Morpheus placed a dream upon his head. Straightway then the Knight did dream that lovely Una falsely loved another and but left to him the dangers of delivering her parents. Again and once again that troublous dream essayed to make him leave the maid. Yet was he true himself, too true to disbelieve another. Naught could make him doubt the pure and loyal faith of Una. Then did Archimago, taking that same sprite who brought the dream from Morpheus, make him by his arts appear to be a knight. To him he brought the sprite who wore the form of Una. Waking then his guest, the wizard bade him rise and come to see his lady holding secret converse in the darkness with her lover. Amazed, the Red Cross Knight went with the aged man. But when he saw together that sprite so like to Una and the one so like a knight, he knew not what to think. Within himself he struggled until the evening star had spent its lamp in highest heaven. Bewildered and tormented, he held the false for true. Fair Una must be false! She must be false to him! He told the dwarf his tale. The dwarf believed it also and they fled the place together, leaving Una there deserted.

Now when the rising sun touched highest hills with light, fair Una did arise to seek her Knight and dwarf. Alas! She found them gone, and knew no reason why. Weeping, she set forth. She rode to seek her Knight. She searched and found him not. In every hill and dale she searched and found him not.

Flying, ever flying before his wrathful thoughts, the Knight pursued his way. And so it chanced he met a huge-limbed Saracen, who bore upon his shield his name of *Sansfoy* writ. Beside him rode a Lady clad in scarlet cloth, her head in splendid headdress, her palfrey decked with tinsel, her bridle ringing merrily a chime of golden bells. This Lady bade her swain attack the Red Cross Knight. Forward sprang Sansfoy. The other couched his spear; they met in shock so furious that both the horses staggered. Then each knight drew his sword. Fire flew from stricken shields as from an anvil beat with hammers. Therewith the Red Cross Knight struck Sansfoy such a blow he clove clean through his head.

"Mercy!" cried the Lady. With tears she now declared that she was one Fi-des'sa, most faithful of good maids. By force she had been taken, so her story ran, by that dead knight, Sansfoy, who with his wicked brothers, Sansloy and Sansjoy, was ever working evil. "Much relieved am I," she cried, "to be delivered from Sansfoy!" Deceived now by her beauty and her simple dainty ways, the Knight believed her tale. He bade her journey on with him protected by his care. Yet all she said was false. No faithful maid, Fidessa, but Du-es'sa, false, was she. And Sansfoy, faithless knight, had been her chosen lover. Yet since the Red Cross Knight had all too easily believed the evil spoken of Una, fair falsehood took her place to work the Knight much woe.

The Knight and Lady now did journey on together until they reached a place

> Where grew two goodly trees, that fair did spread
> Their arms abroad with gray moss overcast.

Here lighting from their steeds, they sought refreshment of the shade and to the foolish Knight this dame did now appear the fairest ever seen. To make a garland for her head, he plucked a leafy bough from one of those two trees. Lo, from the wound there trickled little drops of blood. A voice cried from the tree: "O spare to tear my side! And fly, Sir Knight! Fly far, lest that befall you here that here imprisoned me." The Knight's hair rose in horror! But groaning deep, the voice cried: "I was

once a man! Duessa, false, beguiled me so I knew not which
was fairer, she or my own maid.
Bewildered by her magic, I cast
my true love off. Her then by
enchantment Duessa made a
tree. With that false dame I
journeyed until the year turned
round. But when came that one
day when witches must appear
in their true guise at last, I saw
Duessa bathing! I saw her as
she was, a filthy, foul old hag,
misshapen, monstrous, hideous.
I tried to flee her power; but
she, in jealous anger, changed
me likewise to a tree. O fly, Sir Knight! Fly far lest that false
dame beguile you, too!"

Much was the good Knight moved by this unhappy tale. He
closed with clay the wound that he had given the tree, yet did he
never guess that she, the lady with him, who called herself Fidessa,
was in truth Duessa, the enchantress of the tale. In show of pity
now, the Lady swooned away. Concerned for her distress, the
Knight did chafe her hands and bring her to her senses. Then
he led her from the place. Long now they journeyed forward
till at last they saw before them a splendid castle rising. On
the highway leading to it many people traveled, rich ones going
toward it but ever those returning only wretched beggars, and
though it was full lofty with many splendid towers, it stood on
weak foundations so it shook in every wind.

Full eagerly Duessa bade her knight to hurry thither. They
entered through the gate and sought the lofty hall. On every side
were splendor, rich array and costly dress, and on a golden throne,

in gorgeous royal robes, there sat the maiden queen, disdainful,
haughty, proud. She kept her eyes raised high nor looked so low
as earth and gazing in a mirror, she watched her self-loved face.
Proud Lu-ci-fer'a was she, usurper, despot, tyrant. Disdainfully
she greeted Duessa and her Knight. Scarce did she bid them
rise as they did reverence before her. Duessa minded not. She
loved the pomp and show; but now the Red Cross Knight, in spite
of this display, thought all this glory vain and that great Princess
far too proud.

Arising from her throne the Queen called for her coach. She
sallied forth, all brightness, all ablaze with glorious glitter; but
lo, when she had climbed into her golden coach what strange
steeds bore that chariot! Six strange beasts there were and on
the back of each rode one of six strange counsellors that governed
with evil the realm. First rode a sluggish, lazy, idle wight in

black monk's robe, astride a slothful ass. Then came a gluttonous fellow, eating, drinking, on a swine. Wall-eyed, the third advisor rode, jealous, on a goat. The fourth, thin, spare and threadbare, a greedy miser was, who sate astride a camel loaded down with gold; and next an envious man upon a ravenous wolf. Last rode one on a lion, his stern eyes pale as ashes, yet hurling fiery sparks. And driving all those steeds, there sat upon the wagon beam Satan with a whip to lash the lazy team.

In such array they marched to sport in flowery fields though underneath their feet lay skulls and bones of men that in that land had come to grief. Duessa rode beside the Queen, her head held high with pride, but that good Knight fell back, withdrawing from vain joys of unfit fellowship.

When unto that proud palace they returned again, they found a knight arrived whose name was called Sansjoy. This knight espied the shield of Sansfoy, his dead brother, borne by Una's dwarf, and loud he cried for vengeance. The Red Cross Knight then fiercely encountered this Sansjoy. With clash of arms they fought until the Queen commanded that they should desist, and on the following day contend in equal lists for that disputed shield.

But when the darksome night had drawn her coal black curtain over brightest sky and all were gone to rest, up rose Duessa from her couch and sought Sansjoy in secret. She told him how she hoped that he would kill this Knight who thought himself her lover and take her for his dame, since next to his dead brother, she loved him, Sansjoy.

IN SHINING ARMOR

Sansjoy arose with morning. He donned his sun-bright arms and went forth to the fray. Beneath a stately canopy, Queen Lucifera sat. Near by Duessa was and on a tree the shield.

And now a trumpet shrilling bade the knights begin the battle. The Saracen was strong; his blows like hammers fell. He struck the Red Cross Knight so hard a blow he swooned. In joy Duessa cried: "Thine are the shield, Sansjoy, the shield and I and all!" Hearing her loved voice though not the words she spoke, the Knight woke from his swoon. With quickening faith he struck. He forced Sansjoy, defeated, to fall down on his knees. But when he raised his sword to deal the blow of death, a magic cloud arose and hid his foe from sight. In vain the Red Cross Knight struck out to reach Sansjoy. By magic he was hidden. By magic he was saved. Then swiftly to the victor the false Duessa came with great pretence of joy. The trumpets sounded victory and heralds brought the shield unto the Red Cross Knight. But secretly Duessa wept until the even-tide; then did she seek Sansjoy and minister unto him.

But now the wary dwarf in dungeons of the palace found wretched creatures languishing, they who had sought the House of Pride in hopes to share its riches, yet were by that proud Queen cast off in misery to die. Awakening thus to knowledge of the nature of the place, the Red Cross Knight did flee. Duessa, coming back from ministrations to her lover, found her erstwhile Knight had gone. Full loath to loose him from her power, she mounted her swift palfrey to ensnare him once again.

Meantime, through long, sad days, fair Una went her way. Through woodland and through waste-land, she sought her Knight in vain. At last, quite wearied out, she lighted from her beast and laid her limbs to rest, far from the sight of men.

> Her angel face
> As the great eye of heaven shinèd bright,
> And made a sunshine in the shady place.

Beneath a tree she lay until a ramping lion issued, rushing from the wood. With gaping mouth, full greedily, he bore down on the maid. But when he was drawn nigh, all couched to seize his prey, he sudden stayed himself. Before her maiden loveliness, his furious rage did fall. He fell before her feet and licked her hands with fawning tongue. And now when Una marked how this great, raging beast, the Lord of all that forest, yielded up his pride before her womanhood, her heart gan melt in great compassion. She stroked his shaggy hide with purest tenderness and when she sate her palfrey to continue on her quest, the lion would not leave her, but journeyed by her side.

And now whom did she meet but one who seemed to be the long lost Knight she sought? In joy she rode to meet him. In relief her heart did melt. In joy he seemed to greet her. With fair words and good reasons he explained why he had left her and they journeyed on together. But in truth this man who seemed to be the Red Cross Knight was none but Archimago who had changed his form by magic, setting out to seek fair Una and once more have power of her. They rode in gladsome talk until upon a sudden, Sansloy came down the road, third of those wicked brothers. He, seeing here the arms of that same Red Cross Knight, who had destroyed Sansfoy, charged forward at full speed. Full loath was Archimago to meet that savage charge, yet by the lady's presence, he was pricked thereto. Blows thundered, sabres flashed and Archimago fell. Sansloy unlaced his helmet and to his own surprise disclosed no Red Cross Knight but Archimago, the magician. Turning then, Sansloy dragged Una from the ass. Now sprang the lion forward. Alas! he could not stand against the Paynim's sword. With lifted blade Sansloy did pierce that faithful heart. He seized the helpless maid and bore her, will or nill, away upon his courser. Full piteously she screamed.

But far within the wood a troop of Fauns and Sa'tyrs danced on hairy goats' legs, and while they were full busy with their merry sylvan games they heard the maiden's shrieks. They ran whence came that cry. And when Sansloy beheld that rude, misshapen rabble, the like of which in all his life he had not seen before, he got upon his steed and flew away in fright.

Astounded at the beauty and the woful plight of Una, these rustic folk, in wonder, fell prostrate at her feet. Dancing, shouting, singing, they led her from the place, they strewed her way with branches, they crowned her with fair garlands.

> And all the way their merry pipes they sound,
> That all the woods with doubled echo ring;
> And with their hornèd feet do wear the ground,
> Leaping like wanton kids in pleasant Spring.

They brought her to Sylvanus, their King, within his arbor.

And when that king beheld the loveliness of Una, he scarce could think her mortal. He deemed her some great goddess. Then came the wood-nymphs, too. All wondering at her beauty, they fell upon their knees and offered her their worship as Goddess of the Wood. In vain did Una try to teach those simple creatures that she was but a woman and no source of power divine. Her words were useless quite; for when she did restrain their zeal from worshipping her as goddess they bowed before that snow-white ass and made of it a god.

In time unto the wood there came a noble knight, Sir Satyrane by name. He, on a certain day when all the Fauns and Satyrs had gone to serve Sylvanus, helped the Lady Una make her way beyond those sylvan glades and woodlands. Yet even as they journeyed Sansloy appeared again. He fell upon Sir Satyrane and furious was the combat. Una fled in fright. Alone again she wandered in search of her good Knight.

But that good Knight, now fleeing from the palace with the dwarf, had again been overtaken by the false Duessa, who still called herself Fidessa. She found him in a glade beside a bubbling fountain where cheerful birds made music and through the trembling leaves a little wind did play. Deceiving, she reproached him for leaving her in flight. Deluding with feigned sweetness, she won his heart again. Seated side by side, they dallied in the wood. But now, as false Duessa knew, the fountain there was magic. Whoever drank thereof lost all his strength and force. She watched as on the brink the Knight lay down and drank.

Eftsoons his force gan fail and he grew weak as water. Yet still he paid his foolish idle court to false Duessa. And now he heard loud bellowing, and ere he could don armor, Or-go'gli-o appeared, a giant towering up so high he seemed to threat the skies. With strides of this great giant, the very ground did groan and in his hand as weapon he bore a shaggy oak.

When he espied the Knight the Giant gan advance. The

IN SHINING ARMOR

Knight prepared for battle; yet all disarmed he was and eke so faint he scarce could stand. The Giant struck with fury; the Knight leapt swift aside, yet did the very wind raised by the Giant's blow have power to hurl the Red Cross Knight senseless to the ground. Duessa begged the Giant to make his foe his slave and take her as his dame. Thereunto agreeing, Orgoglio took the Knight and cast him in a dungeon. To Duessa he gave gold and purple rich to wear and for a steed to ride upon a beast with seven heads, its scales of iron and brass.

When thus the woful dwarf beheld his master fall, he took his shield and spear and quickly fled away. But as he ran at last he met fair Una likewise fleeing. Repentant now, he told of what had chanced since he had left her. Fair Una grieved to hear, yet still went forward firmly to find her own true Knight.

It chanced then that she met a man in glittering armor and golden dragon-helmet. Prince Arthur was his name and when he heard her tale he bade her be of cheer, he vowed he would not quit her till he had met Orgoglio and set free her captive Knight. They sought the Giant's castle. Prince Arthur's squire blew mightily upon a magic horn and at that sound the castle quaked to its foundations. Every door sprang open and the Giant in a bower, dallying with Duessa, rushed forth in dismay. Duessa followed savage, high mounted on her beast, whose every head did flame with fiery blazing tongue.

Lifting high aloft his dreadful oak-tree club, the Giant aimed a blow. Prince Arthur leapt aside so that the mighty mace fell deep embedded in the earth. And while the Giant bending, sought to free the club, Prince Arthur with his shining blade, clove his left arm off. With rage the Giant bellowed and Duessa with her beast rushed in to his defence. Ramping, all the heads of that great beast did flame. But Arthur's squire did meet him with his single sword. Then false Duessa sprinkled poison on the squire so strength and courage fled and he fell helpless to the

ground. Turning now Prince Arthur came to save his squire. He smote with his stout blade one head of that dread monster; he clove it to the teeth. Thereat the creature raged; he scourged the empty air, he lashed with his long tail; he would have thrown his rider, had Orgoglio not come to her. With force of his two arms now joined in that one left, the Giant raised his club and smote Prince Arthur to the ground. Yet in the Prince's fall the veil that until now had covered from sight his shield was suddenly rent asunder. And lo, from that bright shield such dazzling brightness shone, it smote the Giant's eyes, he let his arm fall down and likewise that foul beast was blinded by the light. Affrighted in its brilliance, the monster fell to earth and yielded himself conquered. Duessa screamed aloud and once again Orgoglio sought to raise his mace. In vain! In flashing beams from that bright gleaming shield he had no power to strike. And so Prince Arthur slew him.

Duessa sought to flee but that light-footed squire gave chase and brought her back, while Una and Prince Arthur entered in the castle. In foulest cavern dark, they found the Red Cross Knight. Deep sunken were his eyes; his cheeks were thin and bare, his arms but skin and bones. Yet Una seeing him, flew unto him with joy despite his dolorous look. "Welcome, my lord," she cried. "Welcome in weal or woe!" And Arthur showed the Knight where now his foe lay dead and that false dame stood conquered, the root of all his woes.

"Now is it in your power," quoth he, "to let her live or die."

"It were a shame," quote Una, "to avenge ourselves on one so weak as she. Despoil her of her robe and let her fly, I pray!"

They stripped her of her robe and there she stood revealed,

a loathly, wrinkled hag, gums toothless and head bald.

> "Such then," said Una, "as she seemeth here,
> Such is the face of falsehood; such the sight
> Of foul Duessa, when her borrowed light
> Is laid away, and counterfeiting known."

To hide her shame Duessa ran off to rocks and caves; but Una and the knights abode within the castle and those two knights swore friendship ere in good time they parted.

Then Una and her Knight once more set forth to save that ancient King and Queen from duress of the dragon. But as they went their way, they saw a knight, disheveled, his hair on end for horror, a rope about his neck. He cried as they came nearer that he fled from dark despair. He and a friend, he said, had failed in some great quest and as they were returning they had met with an old man. Subtle, cunning, the old man had argued they were failures. Never could they hope that they might still achieve and so might better die. With wily words the man had filled their souls with such despair that one of these poor knights had seized a knife and slain himself, while he, who fled with staring eyes, had even had the rope about his neck to hang himself, when from the evil enchantment of those words he fled away.

"I will crush this sorcerer who poisons with despair!" So quoth the Red Cross Knight. Yet when he found the man within a doleful cave, the man made no defence. He only spake his gloomy words. He spake of this world's evils—sickness, fear, old age, labor, sorrow, strife, hunger, pain, and loss. Subtly, too, he gan to mind the Red Cross Knight of all the evils he had done, of how for that false witch he had deserted his true love, had lived in pride and sloth, all barren of good deeds. So might he better die. Those poisoned words in time possessed with full bewilderment the mind of that good Knight. He saw himself as hopeless, useless, sinning, worthless, deserving only punishment by the Almighty's law. The hideous old man made offer of a dagger. Seizing then the weapon, the Knight did lift his hand to stab his own sad breast. But Una, undeceived, snatched from his hand the dagger. "Fie, fie, faint-heart!" she cried. "Is this the way thou goest forth to battle with the dragon and save my captive parents? Let not devilish thoughts dismay thy constant spirit! Arise, Sir Knight! Arise and leave this cursed place!"

So forth they rode in haste and Una, seeing now how weak in soul he was for that he dwelt in mind on all the evil he had done, did take him to a fair and pleasant house nearby, that there he might recover. Through a narrow gate they entered and from the spacious court, a squire, sincere and simple, led them to the Lady Celia, the good mistress of the place. In modest guise she welcomed Una and her Knight. Then, arm in arm, into the hall there came two lovely virgins, the Lady Celia's daughters, their countenances demure and full of modest grace. Fidelia, eldest daughter, was arrayed in lily white, her face like crystal shone; Speranza, youngest daughter, was clad in heavenly blue. With glowing words of kindness these two maids did greet the strangers and when with one night's sleep the Knight was well refreshed, fair Una begged Fidelia to talk with him and save him from the gloom of his despair. And so the shining maid talked glowingly of grace, of justice, and free will, and how despite all sins that may be in the past, men may by full repentance and the fullness of their faith, have power to move great mountains and be useful still to men. Then came to him Speranza with her steadfast upward gaze. Speranza gave him hope that it was not too late by good deeds to redeem the evil of his past. And when they two had spoken, Una led her Knight to Celia's loveliest daughter, the beautiful Charissa. Upon an ivory chair with turtledoves nearby the fair Charissa sat and all about her arms, her chair, a multitude of babes went climbing, sprawling, clinging, playing merry sports that filled her full of joy to see. In

tenderest wise she cared for all these little ones. Full tenderly she spoke the joys of charity—

> Of love, and righteousness and well to done,
> And wrath and hatred warily to shun.

And when through joys of that good house the Knight was full of hope, of love, and great good will, Charissa called to her an ancient Dame of Mercy and bade her guide the Knight upon his further way. They mounted till they reached a Chapel on a hill, and near thereto a hermitage, where dwelt an aged man who far from worldly cares, now spent his days and nights in thought of holy things. And when the Knight had fasted and given himself to prayer, the old man led him up unto the highest height of that high mount of his.

> From thence, far off, he unto him did show
> A little path that was both steep and long,
> Which to a goodly city led his view,
> Whose walls and towers were builded high and strong.
> The City of the Great King, hight it well
> Wherein eternal peace and happiness doth dwell.

Which, when he saw so full of beauty and of light, the Knight did cry: "O let me not turn back into the world, whose joys are all so fruitless. Let me go, I pray thee, unto that Heavenly City and forever rest in peace!"

The old man shook his head. "As yet that may not be! Thou must first, my son, do thy work on earth. Go and slay the dragon, set the maiden's parents free. For only when with steadfastness thou hast performed thy work and labor on the earth, doth that fair city wait thee. Go forward on thy quest!"

And now, well purged of sin, his heart rejoicing, full of faith, of hope and charity, and in his thoughts high visions of that life of joy to win, the Knight fared forth with Una.

Eftsoons they came upon the brazen tower where that old King and Queen were held in durance by the dragon, and all at once they heard a hideous roaring sound as on a great hill's sunny side they saw the monster come. Half flying and half footing, he drew near his foe, casting much wide shadow under his huge wings. Like two bright shields his eyes did burn. They sparkled living fire. The Knight made at him fiercely, but the beast turned swift about and with his tail swept horse and rider to the ground.

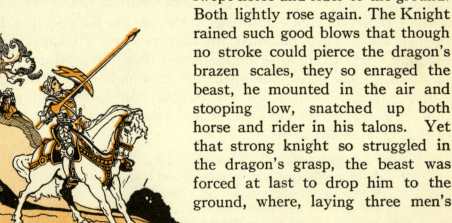

Both lightly rose again. The Knight rained such good blows that though no stroke could pierce the dragon's brazen scales, they so enraged the beast, he mounted in the air and stooping low, snatched up both horse and rider in his talons. Yet that strong knight so struggled in the dragon's grasp, the beast was forced at last to drop him to the ground, where, laying three men's

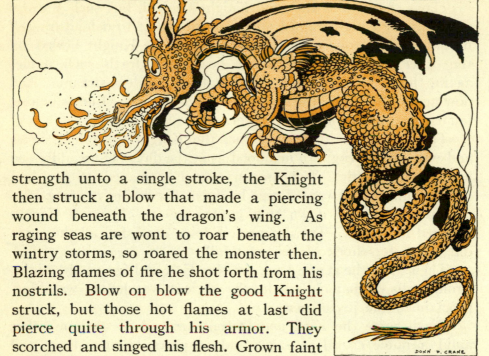

strength unto a single stroke, the Knight then struck a blow that made a piercing wound beneath the dragon's wing. As raging seas are wont to roar beneath the wintry storms, so roared the monster then. Blazing flames of fire he shot forth from his nostrils. Blow on blow the good Knight struck, but those hot flames at last did pierce quite through his armor. They scorched and singed his flesh. Grown faint and weary in such heat, worn out with toil and wounds, the Knight was by that dragon's tail hurled deep into a well.

And now with breast expanded, clapping mightily his wings, the dragon did proclaim his victory in the battle. Yet all night long fair Una ever watched and prayed, and when the morning came, behold! The Red Cross Knight sprang whole from out that magic well with life and strength renewed.

Amazed at sight of him, his foe stood still in doubt. The Knight then dealt his crest so sore a blow it cleft the skull. The beast, loud-yelling, towered and bore the Knight to earth, then with his sting he pierced his shoulder. There did that vile sting stick, nor could it be got out. The good Knight raised his blade and cleft the monster's tail so that the stump alone remained within his shoulder. Breathing furious flames, the dragon with his claws then seized the good Knight's shield, but such a storm of blows the Knight rained on the dragon that to defend himself he had to loose one claw. Smiting hard, the Knight hewed off the other claw. Raging now the beast sent forth such flames again, the Knight perforce retired and fell beside a stream. And now again full noisily the dragon boasted victory. But as before, fair Una spent the night in prayer.

Thus when the morning came, the Knight, refreshed, arose and with full strength of manhood as in the days before addressed him to the battle. The dragon waxed dismayed to see him thus again. With wonted rage he opened wide his yawning jaws to seize him. But down that gaping mouth the good Knight plunged his sword. The dragon fell down dead and all the earth did groan for shock of his great fall.

Then came the gentle Una, praising God and her good Knight. From walls of that old castle, the ancient watchman, watching, proclaimed the joyful news.

Forth came the King and Queen, arrayed in antique robes amid a noble crowd of sages and of peers. Before them tall young men bore fresh green laurel boughs; and in their wake, all dancing, a crew of comely virgins came with tinkling timbrels bearing flowery garlands while children, sporting gaily, made music all the way.

They crowned fair Una with their garlands; they laid their laurel boughs before the good Knight's feet, the whiles that hoary King gave thanks and princely gifts unto the slayer of the dragon and once again the daughter was held in fond embrace by father and by mother. With trumpets and with clarions were Una and her Knight led up within the castle while before them all the people strewed the streets in joy with costly robes and garments. Within the old gray castle the King gave gentle Una as bride unto her Knight and so in happiness did end that long and toilsome quest.

IN SHINING ARMOR

Mar'ko, the Champion of Serbian Liberty

A Tale of the 14th Century from Ballads of the Yugo Slavs

IN THE days of Stephen, the Tsar, there came an end for a time, to years upon years of war in the blood-stained mountains of Serbia. Yugoslavia, Bulgaria, almost all the land to the walls of Is-tan-bul', became at last united under the rule of Stephen. With churches and fair white palaces Stephen adorned his cities. Under him learning flourished and great was the glory of Serbia. But already there rose in the East a dark cloud foreboding evil. A Moslem army of Turks seized land on Serbia's threshold and from that unhappy hour the advancing power of the Turk over-shadowed the Balkans. Then, too, Serbian nobles, powerful and ambitious, sought to throw off Stephen's rule, to play the game of statecraft each for his own good alone; and foremost among these, Vu-ka'shin, an able man and unscrupulous, ruled with too great power the southern lands of the Tsar.

Now Vukashin and his wife, the fair and good Ye-vro-si'ma, had two sons and a daughter. Of these the greatest was Mar'ko. Gigantic in strength and spirit, honest and frank of heart, Marko was taught wisdom from ancient books of the Slavs in the white church of Archpriest Ne-del'ko.

Great was the bond of love that bound Marko unto his mother; but the youth's frank and generous spirit aroused in the heart of his father jealousy, fear, and hate.

One day the Archpriest Nedelko, teaching the boy, spake thus: "Kings and tsars, my son, are the most important people in the world."

"Nay," Marko answered. "More important than kings, more important than tsars, are the orphans and poor of the land!"

"A man should love God," said Nedelko, "and he should honor his King."

Marko, hero of the Yugo Slavs, has been splendidly carved in stone by their sculptor, Meštrović, whose statues adorn some of our American cities, notably the gigantic horsemen on the lake front in Chicago. (Vol. III, p. 194.)

"A man should honor his King only in case the King reigns as one just and honorable!" Thus with surprising words the youth replied to his teacher. And when the Archpriest told Vukashin what Marko, his son, had said, the father was in a rage. So great was the fury upon him that Marko fled from the palace.

For three years now on the plains Marko worked as a herdsman tending fire-breathing horses and when his service was over, he was minded to test the steeds to choose him a horse for battle. Seizing each horse by the tail he tried to see if its strength could withstand the power he exerted to swing it over his head. Not a horse could withstand him until he came to Sha'rats, the wonder-horse of the herd. Sharats he could not lift. He could not with all his strength swing Sharats over his head. And so with great joy he chose this dappled-gray steed for his horse. The two became fast friends; they shared the same food and wine and Marko gave unto Sharats the half of all that he had.

Fame of the exploits of Marko, his honesty and his strength, spread rapidly through the land till they came to the ears of Tsar Stephen. Then Stephen wrote to Vukashin saying: "Send me your son. I need men of knowledge and valor to protect the Serbian realm."

But Vukashin feared that Marko would never further his father's ambitious and evil schemes; and so he replied to Stephen: "Marko is a wild youth of uncontrollable will; he will only shame me, his father, and displease you, the Tsar."

Nevertheless, Tsar Stephen replied to Vukashin bluntly: "I want such a hero as Marko. Send him here unto me."

IN SHINING ARMOR

Under lofty towers of the castle, out of the marble courtyard, Marko rode forth on Sharats. Glittering his golden armor, glittering the points of light from the golden wing on his cap! Glittering the cloth of gold beneath the great black bearskin on which the hero rode, glittering its golden tassels sweeping the very ground. From her home on a neighboring height, Yevrosima came down to bid her son farewell.

"O my dear son," she said as he bowed his head to her blessing. "In the white city of Pri'zren you will meet all the Serbian heroes. Take your place with those who have helped the Tsar give us peace and build up the Serbian land."

Marko then in silence kissed his mother's hand; she kissed his cheeks and his brow and her sorrowing tears fell fast. As he rode down over the plain she watched until he was naught save a gleam and a flash in the distance. Mounting, then, her high tower she followed him still with her eyes. One last glitter of light and there on the far horizon, over the rim of the hills, he was lost at last to her sight.

Marko is in Stephen's palace. Never before has he seen such wonders of gold and silver, such pearls and shining of gems. He

has kissed the hand of the Tsar; he has kissed the hand of Ro-xan'da, the Empress of the realm; he has taken his place with the heroes in the imperial household of Stephen. He has sworn with heroic friends, Mi'losh and the winged Re'lya, the fast vows of brotherhood. Now goes their fame through the land, the fame of their deeds and their friendship. Wherever the minstrel twangs the single string of his gousle', he sings of the exploits and friendship of Marko, Milosh and Relya.

But now the Tsar Stephen lay dying. One young son he had, a child of eleven years, and the youth of the lad lay heavy on the mind of the dying Tsar. Calling to him Vukashin he said: "My dear vowed-brother, I leave to you U'rosh, my son. Rule for him seven years; but when the eighth year comes and Urosh shall be eighteen, give over to him the realm."

So Stephen was gathered to his fathers, Marko went home to Pri'lip and Vukashin ruled the land. He ruled for seven years; he ruled for eight long years; he ruled for nine long years. Never did he intend to give back the realm to Urosh. Ever his power grew greater and heavier grew his taxes, till all the people groaned and despair lay dark on the land. Then in the sixteenth year Urosh went to his mother asking his father's heritage. The sorrowing Empress answered:

"Nine years ago, my son, the kingdom should have been yours; but Vukashin will not yield it!"

So Urosh wrote to Nedelko, he who was Stephen's confessor and had been with him on his deathbed. He, if any, should know what had been Stephen's will. Urosh begged him to state who was really heir to the realm.

But others, too, claimed the throne. Vukashin had two crafty brothers, tyrants and despots both. Those three brothers had met. On the broad plain of Ko-so'vo, they had pitched their tents, quarreling among themselves as to who should be Tsar in the land. As the messenger of Urosh went quietly off to Nedelko, messengers from the three brothers galloped on the same errand. Boldly they dashed through the streets. Impiously they hammered on the sacred door of the church where Nedelko was serving the mass.

"Come at once, O Nedelko, to the field of Kosovo," they shouted. "You shall give judgment there as to whom Stephen left the kingdom. Come in haste, we bid you, or you shall lose your head!"

"Wait, ye impatient without!" So sadly spake Nedelko. "You interrupt holy service!" Nor did he come from the church until the service was over.

"My children," then he said, "it is true that I gave the Tsar the last rites of holy sacrament, but I never talked to him about politics or the kingdom. I talked to him of his sins. Go you to Marko, the King's son, there where he lives in white Prilip. He served as secretary unto the good Tsar Stephen; and Marko will tell you the truth, for no one he fears save God."

It is not with noise and threats that the messengers dare approach Marko. Respectful and quiet of mien, they climb the steep path to the palace. Humbly they state their mission unto the mother of Marko. Called by the good Yevrosima, Marko comes forth to greet them.

"O Marko, the King's son," they say. "The mighty lords have gathered on the broad field of Kosovo. There they are debating who shall be Tsar in the land. Come to Kosovo, we beg you, and tell them from Stephen's papers who is the rightful heir."

Marko saddles his Sharats; he loads the horse with his papers.

"Tell them the truth, my son," the good mother says in parting.

Marko comes to Kosovo. He draws near his father's tent.

"Now are things well for me," Vukashin says to himself. "Marko, my son, is judge. He will give me the throne, that he may inherit it later and rule as Tsar himself."

But Marko says nothing in greeting. He rides past his father's tent. And likewise in silence he rides past the tents of his two crafty uncles. Up to the fourth tent he goes, the white tent timidly raised by Urosh among the contenders. Urosh runs forth to greet him.

"Good it is, Marko, my brother, to see you here," he cries, "for you will tell us truly who is the heir to the kingdom."

Then the two men embraced and Marko went in with Urosh and spent the night in his tent. With morn came the voice of the bell, the great bell in the church calling the people to worship. Into the House of God went Marko and the four princes. Splendid was the service; gorgeous the altar screen with jewel-like paintings of saints, before them small lamps burning; and high over all, gigantic, the Last Judgment in a picture, there to remind Serb princes that they must rule with justice. Worshipers lighted the candles; they placed them around the church. The whole building blazed with light, studding the sacred darkness. For hours the service continued. Standing, the princes chafed, impatient for Marko's decision, and when the service was ended, they fared forth into the open. Flinging themselves into chairs around the several tables placed there in the open under the shade of the trees, they eagerly sipped their brandy. All eyes were fixed on Marko. Before them he spread out his papers, old records of good Tsar Stephen.

"King Vukashin, my father," he said. "Is your kingdom too small? Is it small? May it then become waste since you try to steal another's realm!

"And you, the eldest of my uncles, is your land too small? Is it small? May it then become waste since you try to steal another's realm!

"And you, the youngest of my uncles! Is your land too small? Is it small? May it then become waste since you try to steal another's realm! Plainly the records say that Urosh is the heir.

The crown goes from father to son, from Stephen down to Urosh, and so will it continue to the very end of time."

Raging, Vukashin leaped up. Drawing his sword, he lunged, frantic with wrath, at his son. But what man will fight his father? Yea, though he know himself stronger, what son will fight his sire? Marko turned from the mad man. Fleeing, he ran for his life. Three times around the church Vukashin chased his son. Nowhere appeared a refuge. But when for the fourth time Marko passed the door of the church there came from within a voice.

"Run into the church, O Marko," thus spake the voice within. "Otherwise you will perish for the sake of the truth of God."

Miraculously the gates of the House of God swung open. Marko entered in haste. Again were the portals closed by that same miraculous hand. Dashing against the gates, Vukashin drove his dagger up to the hilt in the wood. But lo, as he did so, blood trickling drop by drop, bespattered the sacred door. Awakening at sight of the blood from his wild frenzy of rage, Vukashin came to himself.

"Woe is me!" he cried, "for I have destroyed my son!"

But the same voice cried from within:

"Nay, King Vukashin, nay! Marko, thy son, is safe. Thou hast slain an angel of God!"

Then raged the King more than ever, cursing Marko, his son.

"May you have neither grave nor descendants! May your soul not pass from your body until you have bowed the knee to the infidel son of the Turk!"

But Urosh heaped blessings on Marko.

"O Marko, God help you!" he cried. "May your face be bright in council! May your sword be sharp in battle! And may your fame endure while sun and moon remain!"

Not with Marko's just judgment did the troubles of Serbia end; for Vukashin kept up his intrigues, and discords disturbed the land. King Urosh, alack, was weak. Good-natured and sweet of temper, he was not one able to thwart the plots of his wily foe. Vukashin had Urosh murdered and ruled again in his stead.

Now during all this time Marko was living at home in white Prilip. Yevrosima, his mother, acted as hostess for him, watching over her son. Rather she chose to live across the well-paved courtyard on the twin peak opposite Marko, with its far view of the sea and its mile of encircling walls, than now to dwell in Skadar in the palace of her husband.

What love could Marko have, what agreement with such a sire? Nothing he knew of his plans; little he knew of his life. In the meantime, the Serbs to the north had chosen King Lazar as ruler. In feuds against King Vukashin they rent with disunion the land. The doom of the people was sealed, dark doom of the people of Serbia. For the Turks were now drawing nearer. Vukashin did not oppose them; deep in his heart he hoped they would further his cause in Serbia. But splendid were Turkish arms, rich was the Turkish equipment, weak was the strife-torn Serbia. Too late Vukashin awoke to see that neither he nor yet any other king in all the realm of Serbia would be left in power on his throne by the hordes of the Sultan Murat. In haste he gathered an army, he tried to undo his error; but there by the river Ma-ri'tsa, the Turks in surprise attack fell on the Serbian warriors.

Desperate was the struggle; naught save a land united could have stood against such a foe. Vukashin's brothers died; many a hero fell. Their bodies and those of their steeds rolled down the swollen river, and were scattered for many miles along the sorrowing shore. Red ran the waters with blood; women washing their clothes on the flat stones along the banks miles away from the battle were forced to stop their work till the stream should run clear again.

Far away down the river a Turkish girl at her washing stopped work like all of her sisters. Suddenly, standing idle, she saw King Vukashin, wounded, floating by on the waters. Feebly he called to the girl: "O sister in God, fair maiden! Throw me a rope, I pray you! Pull me out of the river and I will give you due honor."

With difficulty the girl, straining with all her strength, dragged the King from the river and helped him up to the bank. Rich with gold were his garments! Jeweled was his golden sword hilt, worth any three Turkish cities! The eyes of the girl opened wide; for she knew not that he was the King.

But now Vukashin asked: "My sister, O Turkish maiden, who is there in your white house?"

"There is only my aged mother," thus the girl made answer, "and my brother, Mus'taf-a'ga."

"My sister, O Turkish maiden," the wounded King replied. "Go home and fetch your brother to carry me to your white house. You will not go without reward. I have three purses of gold. One I will give to you, the second to your brother, and the third I will keep myself, that I may have wherewithal to pay for the cure of my wounds."

So the maiden ran home to her brother and cried in a great excitement: "O brother, my dear Mustaf-aga, I have dragged from the river a hero wounded and rich. He has three purses of gold and if you will carry him here, one purse he will give to me and one he will give to you. Do not be stern, my brother! Let him not die by the river! Carry him to our white house that we may heal him with care!"

Then the brother went to the river. He saw the wounded hero; he saw the rich clothing and armor; he saw the swelling purses; he saw the golden sword. Dragging his own curved scimitar, he swung it with one swift stroke and cut off the stranger's head. Stripping then the rich clothing, seizing the golden sword, grasping the three full purses, he hurried home with his booty.

"Why have you violated the laws of God?" cried the girl, "and polluted the honor of the family? If God would give me the power I would cut off your head!"

But the brother cared naught for her anger. He went to the Turkish army, there to boast of the sword and all his ill-gotten wealth. Vain and with pompous pride, he strode through the Turkish camp, rejoicing when all who saw him admired his costly weapon and loudly sang of the glory and bravery of Mustaf-aga!

But of all this Marko, the King's son, knew at this time nothing. He had not been called by his father to take part in the battle. Only rumors he heard of Serbia's sad disaster till there came unto him one day a messenger from the Sultan.

"Marko," the Sultan wrote. "Pay heed unto this letter. Your father has perished with his armies. I have taken over the Serb lands. Come you to E-dir'ne and swear allegiance to me!"

"This punishment is visited on me for my father's sins!" cried Marko. "Likewise it is fulfillment of my father's curse on my head."

"My son, submit for now," sadly said Yevrosima. "Await a better time when union shall come to the Serb-lands."

Sadly off to Edirne went the hero Marko; but the Sultan received him kindly. Better it was for him to gain the friendship of Marko, lest he head some great movement to drive the Turks from the land. Moreover, the Sultan ordered his warriors to treat the hero with courtesy and respect.

But now in the Sultan's camp it chanced that the golden sword displayed by Mustaf-aga fell into Marko's hand as it was passed about to be admired by the warriors sitting around the campfires. Vaguely familiar to Marko seemed that costly sword. Three names were engraved upon it. They were the names of Novak, the smith who had made the sword; Vukashin, who carried the sword; and his own name, Marko, the King's son, heir to the throne and the sword!

Calmly Marko addressed the swaggering Mustaf-aga:

"Young man, by what chance came this sword to your hands?"

No dark note foreboding evil did the young Turk read in his tone. He knew not that in the names inscribed in Serbian letters was the sword's whole history writ. Boldly he boasted of how he had slain and robbed the old Serb.

"Why did you kill an old man sick and wounded?" cried Marko. "Why did you not heal him?"

And before the eyes of all, he swung his father's sword and with one well-aimed blow cut off the young Turk's head. Tumult awoke on the instant! Raging, the warriors demanded the head of the insolent Serb. But Marko stood in their midst, gigantic, powerful and calm. No man in all the crowd dared lay a hand upon him. Then came word from the Sultan, summoning Marko to him.

Donning his wild wolf-skin coat and his great savage wolf-skin cap, Marko took his war club and strode to the Sultan's pavilion. Not deigning to take off his boots, he entered the Sultan's presence. Weird, terrifying, wild, his long black mustaches bristling, he advanced to the throne, fiercely swinging his war club.

Fearful, the Sultan rose. Step by step, he retreated until at last he stood cowering against the far wall of the tent. Then reaching into his pocket he brought out a purse full of ducats.

"Take this, Marko," he said, "and drink your fill of wine. Why are you so disturbed?"

But Marko disdained the ducats.

"That was my father's sword," he thundered with mighty thundering. "It was my wounded father Mustaf-aga slew!"

Hearing the truth, the Sultan took refuge in soft words. Marko had done but justice; he held no grudge against him! Let the hero only go home and serve the Sultan there! Let him turn the might of his arm against the foes of the Sultan and keep the peace in the land!

So Marko went back to white Prilip and for a time there was calm. But now in time Marko's mother said to him: "O my dear son, your mother is getting old. No longer can she prepare good food to set before you, nor pour for you the dark wine, nor light your room with the pine torch. Marry, my dear son, that I may see my successor before the day of my death."

And Marko replied: "Dear Mother, I have traveled through nine realms and likewise through the tenth kingdom which is the Turkish Empire. But wherever I have seen a charming and beautiful maiden, she would not have suited you. And wherever I have beheld a maiden suited to you, she was not in mine eyes charming. Only one maid have I seen in the land of the Bulgarians, the daughter of King Shish'man. Lovely, she stood by a cistern. When I saw her my head whirled; the grass seemed to spin around! There is the maid for me, and one, my mother, likewise to be a good daughter to you. Prepare then the sugarcakes that I may go to her father and ask for her hand in marriage."

Gladly Yevrosima made ready for his departure and Marko, when dawn broke fine, rode forth astride of Sharats to journey to far Bulgaria. Gladly the King received him and promised the girl to Marko. Blushing the maid appeared, receiving with joy from Marko the apple and the ring wherewith was pledge of marriage. Three packs full of gifts Marko gave to the bride and unto her mother and sisters. Then he returned to white Prilip to gather the wedding guests, friends gay-clad and faithful to guard the bride on her journey.

Colored banners flying, merry music playing, the cavalcade in time set forth from Bulgaria and in their midst Ye-li'tsa, veiled save for her eyes that shone through narrow slits, her figure quite concealed beneath a costly coat, that no man might behold her until the marriage service in holy church was over. Thus she came to Marko, his beloved bride.

But now when days of happiness lay bright on fair white Prilip, gloom came dark on Serbia; for the Turkish Sultan Murat, satisfied till now with nominal supremacy over the Serbian princes, decided to conquer wholly all the Serbian lands. Therefore, he issued an order that his armies should gather for battle. On Kosovo, Plain of Blackbirds, gathered the Serbian host. Urgent the cry Tsar Lazar sent to the Serbian heroes:

"Who cometh not to Kosovo to battle there with me,
Let nothing grow beneath his hand in fields that he shall till;
Let not the white wheat spring for him, nor vine shoot on the hill."

Kosovo, Plain of Blackbirds, lay white with tents like snow. Of satin and of velvet, Tsar Lazar raised a church.

Knowest thou, O my brother, how the good Tsar Lazar went
With the squadrons of the army to take the Sacrament.
By the fair church on Kosovo the thirty mass-priests stood
For three weeks with the offering of Christ, his flesh and blood.

But where when heroes gather is the greatest of them, Marko? Too late to far white Prilip comes the message of the Tsar. Marko mounts his Sharats; he gallops like the wind. He maddens on his maddened steed with urging and with spur. But there on far Kosovo, the battle has begun. When dawned the fateful day the Serbs rushed forth to battle. Then mingled Turkish turbans and Serb-caps feathered white. But many more in numbers were the Sultan's mighty host.

Ranks of horses and of heroes, spears like a mountain wall
And like the clouds of heaven their banners over all!
To the stirrups of the stallions the brave blood flowed thereby
And the horses of the heroes were all drenched bridle high.

Like living fire flashed Milosh! On the Sultan now he sprang
And over him within his tent, the Serb his swift blade swang;
From midriff to his milk-white throat the Turk alive he rent
And Murat, wordless, bit the ground, there underneath his tent.

Now Turk and Servian lances lie shattered everywhere,
But many more of Christian spears alas were broken there.
Defending good Tsar Lazar in the fury of the fray,
The hero old Yug Bogdan perished on that day.
His nine sons, too, stout champions were slaughtered side by side
Full faithful unto death were they and by each other died.

The mother of Yug's children, she prayed God in her pain
For hawk's eyes and a swan's white wing to fly along the plain,
To see her nine strong children and Yug her lord beside;
And what she prayed for, verily, God granted her that tide.
God gave her eagle eyesight and the swan's swift pinion white;
And on Kosovo plain she found her children slain in fight.

Home to their wives she bore them. From afar they saw her come;
And calling like to cuckoos went out to lead her home.
Then swelled the mother's heart within; her soul was rent in twain
For her children and their father at Kosovo cruelly slain.

On that sad field, Kosovo, the Serbian heroes fell. One and all, save Marko, the Serbian heroes died.

Fatal day, O Serbia, that sad day of Kosovo! For full five hundred years the Turk shall cruelly rule you, for full five hundred

IN SHINING ARMOR

years your minstrels sing this battle, shed their tears in song, and cry their grief in ballads. Back from death to life your gouslars, twanging gousle's, shall call these vanished heroes, holding Serbs in union through sad memories of Kosovo.*

Marko comes at last. He sees the battle done, without him fought and lost. He stands alone of heroes alive among the dead. Save one lone wounded eagle, its wings fast bound with blood, no thing lives on that plain. And Marko grieving sorely, takes the one thing living. He takes it to a mountain and sets it on a tree where gentle rains may wash it that it may fly again. And from a high tower burning he saves the eagle's eaglets. He climbs that burning tower, he brings the eaglets down. He takes them to white Prilip, he keeps them till they fly. Yea, eagles he may serve but living heroes none. Too late he reached Kosovo.

All Marko can do now, alone of Serbian heroes, is to guard his conquered people, save them from the worst oppressions. Oft alone in single combat does he fight the Turkish tyrants. In battle he is wounded and like one time to die, fierce burned by summer sun, with neither shade nor water. There comes, as by a miracle, relief

from some faint shadow. Nearer draws the shadow, broader its relief. Great wings are up above him, overshadowing, cooling. It is the eagle there, the eagle he has saved. Water in her beak the eagle brings to Marko. Perched on Marko's spear, stuck upright in the ground, she keeps her wings outspread, she overshadows Marko till strength again returns and once more he takes heart.

*NOTE: No event has made such a deep impression on the Serbs as the battle of Kosovo, June 15, 1389. It was not until the 19th century that Serbia was delivered from the Turks.

Thenceforward, to white Prilip daily came the poor to seek the aid of Marko. Robbers and oppressors Marko fought and slew, and often from a journey he came home red with blood that stained his clothes and armor.

Now it happened on a day when Marko and Yelitsa sat happily together that Yevrosima spake these words unto her son: "O Marko, son, I pray you, give up your constant warfare. Behold your fertile hills. See how they need your ploughing. What crops you could raise there if you would but stop fighting! Yelitsa, your dear wife, and I, your well-loved mother, are tired of washing clothes all blood-stained from your battles. Take your plough, my son, take now your yoke of oxen and plough up hills and valleys. Set thus a good example of good living to your people and save your wife and mother from washing blood-stained garments."

Marko now, as ever, obeyed his mother's words. He took his plough and oxen and went forth to the fields. But ere he left the castle, he heard disturbing news. A neighboring Serbian city had been plundered by the Turks. With their ill-gotten booty they would soon be passing Prilip. Striding mighty strides, the hero sought the highway. He chose his field for ploughing, he chose the Sultan's highway. Lengthwise with great furrows he ploughed the Sultan's highway. Crosswise with great furrows he ploughed the Sultan's highway. Ditches were his furrows, high hills the soil he turned.

Soon came the Turks exultant, merry with their booty. Seeing then the barrier raised by Marko's ploughing and the hero ploughing still with his gigantic oxen, they called: "O Marko, hearken! Plough not the Sultan's highway."

But Marko answered only: "Do not stop me in my ploughing!"

Once again the soldiers cried: "Plough not the Sultan's highway!" The hero kept on ploughing; he looked nor right nor left. Then angrily the Turks advanced with threats on Marko. Attacking from all sides they came in close upon him. But just as they attacked, the hero caught his plough-pole. High above his head he lifted plough and oxen. With strength as of a giant, he swung the plough and oxen. Like a battle-axe he swung them. Round and round again he whirled them and with each arc he swung he struck a Turk to earth. With blows of that stout ploughshare and the weight of those great oxen, he felled them one and all. They lay heaped on the ground.

"Alack," said Marko then. "My mother and dear wife must still wash blood-stained garments!"

Home he took the booty and he said to Yevrosima: "I could not help it, mother! I have won back for our Serbs the spoils these Turks had stolen. I can now return the booty to those whom they have plundered."

What peace was there for Marko, for a champion of the people? When Easter morning came, before the flush of dawn, before the morning star had risen in the heavens, Marko rose and dressed. He wished to go to service on the far field of Kosovo. Seeing him preparing, Yevrosima said:

"My dear son, you ride forth to take in holy church the sacred Sacrament. This time obey your mother. Enough blood you have shed. You may be tempted still to enter into combat if the foe comes in your path. I beg you then today, do not put on your armor and do not carry weapons. Thus you cannot fight and will not sin again before you reach the church."

Then Marko called his wife and said: "My dear Yelitsa, saddle my good Sharats. Prepare things for my journey, but lay not out for me my battle-axe or sword."

Yelitsa hearkened well. She hearkened and she went. She went to Marko's stable. She saddled and she bridled his beloved Sharats. But yet with loving heart, despite her husband's words, she took his sword and hung it on his saddle bow; she covered sword and saddle with a covering of bearskin. And when her task was ended, she came back to the palace.

"O my lord," she said. "I have made ready Sharats."

Marko mounted Sharats; he bent to kiss Yelitsa. And then Yelitsa whispered: "O my beloved husband, if you find yourself in trouble, feel beneath the bearskin covering. There is something there to save you!"

Thinking only of her beauty, of the joy of her sweet kiss and Easter joy before him, Marko heeded not her words. He kissed her once again and galloped from the courtyard.

Over plains and hills in quiet of the morning he fared forth toward Kosovo. The meaning of glad Easter filled full his bursting heart, the beauty of sweet springtime, of green fields fresh with rains, of life again awakening after winter's sleep. War and blood-stained battle were far then from his mind.

But as the sun rose red, he saw at last Kosovo. With pain his soul was rent. God grant the place might be, at some good time to come, a place of Serbian victory to wipe out that defeat!

And in that moment Marko heard the sound of women wailing, he heard far in the distance doleful cries and lamentations. A cloud of dust appeared and from it there before him emerged a band of Turks, who roughly drove before them a group of Serbian women. Loaded down with chains, the piteous captives came, to be sold into slavery in the mart at Istanbul. And as in their distress they drew near unto Marko, they wailed: "Our brother, save us! You alone can help us!"

A quandary now for Marko! Before him lay the church, the

holy Sacrament. He wished to reach there pure, unstained by human blood. Yet here this hideous thing! How helpless these poor women! A second time, a third, the women wailed their pleadings. No more could Marko stand. He rode up to the Turks, he offered them great sums if they would free the captives. But the Turks replied in scorn: "You beggar, that small sum could never even ransom such an one as you and surely not these women!"

Then Marko offered more; he met with naught but insults. Rage began to mount, his soul within him swelled, he towered as one in fury. Yet wherewith could he fight? He had no weapon with him. He had come unarmed from Prilip. With jeers the Turks rode on, the women grieving still with dolorous cries and weeping. Sorrow as a knife-blade stabbed the heart of Marko. Then sudden on his thoughts there flashed his wife's last words, the words he had not heeded in the kiss of their sweet parting:

"O my beloved husband, if you find yourself in trouble, feel beneath the bearskin. There is something there to save you."

Reaching with his hand beneath the saddle cover, Marko felt with joy the hard, smooth cold of steel. His sword was there beside him! Loosening it in haste, he gave the reins to Sharats; he urged him to full speed! Astounded with the pounding of his unexpected hoof-beats, the Turks looked up and saw him.

"You Turkish curs," he cried, "I offered you great sums to ransom these poor captives. But now with what a ransom shall you let them go!"

He struck as one in fury! His sword flew right and left. Through Turkish skulls it clove, till all that band lay dead. A-flutter those poor women, now weeping tears of joy, beheld their safe deliverance. Then Marko took them home, he led them to their village, gave them back to arms of loved ones. Once again, thereafter, he turned back toward the church.

But how now did he look for services of Easter, his clothes all stained with blood; his horse, too, drenched with blood and flecked with foam of battle! Startled, all the worshipers beheld him as a spectre, terrible, gigantic, a bloody ghost of battle! Protesting, the good priest came from the sacred building to prevent the hero's entrance.

"O Marko, Marko, Marko!" Thus he cried in sorrow. "You cannot even come to holy Easter service without the marks of battle and blood upon your garments!"

Sadly Marko knelt, poured out his tale in sorrow. Hearing then the priest felt change of heart within him.

"This thing is like you, Marko," he nodded his white head. "You could not stay your sword from fighting for the right, though all your soul was yearning to come sinless here on Easter."

And he led the hero gently within the fair white church.

With splendor and with beauty began the Easter service, lamps and candles gleaming, gold and silver coverings on the sacred icons glittering, all the church appearing in the wonderment of light like Heaven come down to earth, the House of God indeed.

Reverently Marko received the Sacrament, reverently he knelt for blessing of the priest.

Then slowly, lost in thought, he left the House of God, he mounted him on Sharats; he went back to white Prilip unto Yevrosima and Yelitsa, his dear wife.

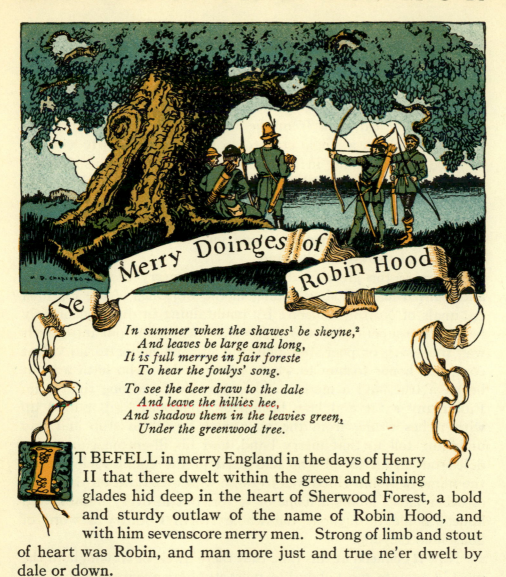

Ye Merry Doinges of Robin Hood

In summer when the shawes[1] be sheyne,[2]
  And leaves be large and long,
It is full merrye in fair foreste
  To hear the foulys' song.

To see the deer draw to the dale
  And leave the hillies hee,
And shadow them in the leavies green,
  Under the greenwood tree.

IT BEFELL in merry England in the days of Henry II that there dwelt within the green and shining glades hid deep in the heart of Sherwood Forest, a bold and sturdy outlaw of the name of Robin Hood, and with him sevenscore merry men. Strong of limb and stout of heart was Robin, and man more just and true ne'er dwelt by dale or down.

Now it was full pity in those days that Justice abode not in courts of law, neither in officers of the Crown; for barons oppressed the poor, the clergy did likewise, and judges and sheriffs of the

Sometime before 1350, while knights in castles told tales of King Arthur, common people in England wove ballads of Robin Hood, doubtless around some outlaw who actually lived and upheld the poor and oppressed against tyranny.   [1]*woods* [2]*beautiful* land used their high office but as a cloak for their corruptions. He who had naught was everywhere ground down beneath the heel of him who had; Justice went limping, blind, and halt, throughout the land, and the King himself in far-off London-town, though he had many a merry tilt with barons and clergy too on this very matter, never came off from the wordy frays with the prize of even so much as a single statute to protect the sturdy yeomen of good old England in their sovereign rights. Thus Justice, beaten out as with cudgels from courts and churches and castles, must e'en go and dwell in the stout hearts of Robin Hood and his bold men of Sherwood Forest, brave yeomen all, each driven from the haunts of men by some villainy that befell them in the name of the law of the land.

There in the greenwood they lived a merry life and a free, and righted many a shortcoming in the workings of the lopsided tribunals of Nottinghamshire by maintaining in due and orderly fashion the superior law of the forest, which, being put into words was this—rich or poor, fair play for all; and honor to no velvet coat, but honor to him to whom honor is due, who hath a stout heart, a true, and a merry, a keen eye, and a strong right arm. Full many a fat and lazy bishop or high-born lord, puffed up with riches wrung from the poor, was forced to stop and pay unwilling toll to that merry band, and his ill-gotten gains were doled out again to all who had need in the countryside. Thus the name of Robin Hood was to those who waxed fat on the fruits of other men's labors a name of terror, but in every humble and honest home throughout the whole North Country a word of household blessing.

Now it chanced at this time that there dwelt in Nottingham the most inveterate, most obdurate, most stubborn enemy of Robin and his men, the right worshipful, right powerful, right proud and haughty Lord High Sheriff of Nottingham. Many a time had good Robin put a spoke in the Sheriff's wheel when he or his friends sought to fleece some innocent squire or yeoman of his goods under fair pretense of right and proper process of law, and many a merry prank had Robin and his men played on that same most worshipful Lord High Sheriff. So had the Sheriff vowed a vow by this and that and all he held most holy to catch bold Robin, have him in chains, and punished with such dire punishment as was meet for a thief and a robber. Yet in all Nottinghamshire could he find not a single man to serve his warrant of arrest on Robin. Too dearly the yeomen and hus-bandmen loved him, and a certain good tinker who but lately set forth to Sherwood Forest to obey the Sheriff's commandment, had fallen, instead, for love of the greenwood and its chief, and joined the band, alack! in place of serving his warrant, whereof that most worshipful Lord High Sheriff had suffered much scorn and laughter of men, and vowed a still more awful vow to have bold Robin Hood yet in irons!

On a bright morn in early spring up rose Robin Hood from his couch of grass and moss beneath the broad-spreading branches of an age-old oak, and plunged his hands and face in the swift-running brook that chattered in saucy ripples over the pebbles. The sun was up and came glimpsing, glancing down through the tangle of leaves overhead, flooding all the velvety greensward with sheen, and waking the cowslips and pink-tipped daisies to laugh back a morning greeting. All the air was fragrant with perfume, and merry with little birds' singing—the lark and the mavis, the cuckoo and throstle. Here a pheasant, his tail feathers tipped with gold, strutted warily down a woodland path; there, a graceful doe and a spotted fawn sprang lightly bounding into the thicket, and everywhere in that deep hidden glade, fringed round about with majestic old oaks, was the stirring joy of the new-risen day. Bold Robin, as he scoured face and neck to a dusky red, caroled lustily a gladsome matin-song.

Soon, stretching and yawning, up rose Robin Hood's men and

came likewise to make themselves clean at the brook. Ere you could say "Jack Robinson," fires were burning away in the wood, flames leaping and crackling in jolly sort, and black kettles boiling and bubbling with savory odor of breakfast a-cooking. In short order the board was spread and sevenscore men all in Lincoln green, with jaunty cock's feathers in their caps, sat merrily down to eat of venison pasty and good white bread in the free and open out-of-doors, with never a wall to shut them in and never a roof save the bright blue sky. There was that huge yokel, Little John, and George-a-green, and Will Stutely, and Gil o' the White Hand, and jolly Friar Tuck and Much, the Miller's son, and Arthur-a-bland, and that sweet singer of ballads, Allen-a-dale, and the dainty dandy, Will Scarlet, who came first to Sherwood Forest clad in scarlet and dallying with a rose, yet had such strength he could tear up a sapling by the roots. There was many another fine fellow, too, whose courage and mettle Robin had made occasion to prove. One and all, those sturdy followers rendered unto Robin Hood and the just and equable law of the greenwood full and implicit obedience.

Breakfast over and done, up rose Robin Hood and quoth: "Lith and listen, my merry men all. Today is the fair in Nottingham-town and the proud Sheriff holdeth there a splendid shooting match. Far and wide through the countryside his messengers have gone to proclaim the contest and thither will go all the best archers of the North Country. He that shooteth the best of all shall win as prize a silver arrow with head and feathers of gold. Now where be archers of greater skill than we of Sherwood Forest? To the shooting match we must go to compete for the prize."

Scarce had Robin Hood finished speaking when up rose that lumbering fellow, Little John, of all the band best loved of Robin.

Though he was called little, his limbs they
were large,
And his stature was seven foot high;
Wherever he came, men quaked at his name,
For soon he would make them to fly.
With a hey down derry, derry down,
And a hey down, down and a down!

"Good master," quoth Little John, "I was yestere'en at the
Blue Boar Inn on Nottingham Road and thither came a stupid
oaf, an archer of the Sheriff's, who being over full of the landlord's best home-brewed ale, made bold to whisper in mine ear
that the Sheriff laughs in his beard and saith to himself, 'Though
I get no man to go to Sherwood Forest and serve my warrant
on Robin Hood, yet by means of my shooting match will I entice
him and his men, and corner them all as easily as foxes in a hencoop.'"

"Ho! Ho!" laughed Robin Hood. "Now buske[1] ye, bowne[2] ye, my merry men all. If such be our friend the Sheriff's intent, we must then more surely than ever hie us to Nottingham-town!"

When the sun was well up in the sky, lo! sevenscore men, their Lincoln green hid beneath sundry disguises, some clad as poor peasants, some as curtal friars, some as tinkers, some as beggars, made off for Nottingham-town. By deep-hidden, tangled wild-wood paths, 'neath lofty green arches of the dusky forest, and over the stile to the highway they went; then down the long, dusty, white road edged with trim, green hedgerows and flowery meadows whence the lark soared singing into the sky; through villages with little thatched cottages, where merry lassies peeped out from the casements, up hill and down dale, till they saw looming up before them and glistening in the sun, the battlements and spires of old Nottingham-town. Here they fell in with a goodly crowd, all going in the same direction, common people afoot, knights and squires on horseback, their ladies in little carts or on gaily curvetting palfries adorned with rich trappings and merry tinkling bells. In the midst of this jolly company, Robin Hood and his men passed on into the town. Here all was hubbub and merriment. On every side were gay booths of colored canvas with floating flags and streamers, wherein cakes and barley sugar and many another good thing were for sale. Tumblers were tumbling on the green, bag-pipes screeching, lads and lassies dancing, and within a ring in the town square a wrestling match was toward. But Robin and his good fellows lingered nowhere. They pressed on out the further gate of the town to the place reserved for the archery contest.

On a green meadow before the old gray wall the range had been set, sevenscore yards and ten in length, and the rows of benches, one above another, that ran along the wall, were filled with all the gaily dressed folk of rank and wealth from the country round about, while opposite them a railing kept back the poor rabble, who

[1]*prepare* [2]*make ready.*

might only stand to look on. At one end of the range, near the great target with its bull's eye and vari-colored circles, rose a lofty seat beneath a splendid canopy, where the Sheriff and his lady were to sit. Robin and his men repaired to a great tent with fluttering banners and there joined the other archers who were gathering to make ready for the contest.

At last and at last, to a mighty fanfare of trumpets that drew all eyes to the town-gate, came issuing forth the proud Sheriff and his lady, all splendidly mounted on horseback and surrounded by a bodyguard of soldiers. They bore themselves right haughtily, and both were clad in marvelous silks and velvets, ermines and swansdown, with chains of gold a-glitter with jewels. No sooner had they taken their seats than a herald sounded three blasts on his silver horn, in answer to which the archers sprang lightly forth to the range mid loud shouts of acclaim from the people.

Such shooting as was done that day had never been seen in the whole North Country before. Now the while William O'Leslie, the Sheriff's head archer, was sending his arrows into the very blue circle that surrounded the bull's eye, and leading all the rest, the Sheriff himself peered squinting about for sight of a single gleam of Lincoln green amongst the archers.

"Ho!" says he, swaggering to his lady. "Methinks that thief, Robin Hood, hath not dared to put his head into my noose. My good William O'Leslie, belike, will win the prize and throughout the countryside men shall proclaim the head archer of the Sheriff of Nottingham to be the best marksman in all the land."

Just then stepped up to the mark a ragged beggar with shaggy brown hair and a black patch over one eye.

"Ho!" says the Sheriff's lady, "Yon rogue is as broad and sturdy as Robin Hood. Look to him well, my love."

"Now, now!" says the Sheriff in scorn, "A lady's fancy doth run away with her like a skittish mare a-start at a shadow. Yon fellow's beard is brown where Robin's is yellow and he hath but one eye. Know well that no man could befool me! Were Robin in this crowd my sharp eye would find him out!"

The stranger took his place, fixed his gray goose shaft in his stout yew bow, took careful aim and twanged the string. Straight flew the arrow to its mark, striking the bull's eye in the very centre! A shout went up from the people, but the Sheriff cried in a rage:

"Now to it, William O'Leslie. Split the beggar's shaft with as good a shot. No better archers live than serve the Sheriff of Nottingham."

But the gray-haired old archer shook his head and flung his quiver back on his shoulder with a mighty rattling of arrows.

"Nay," quoth he. "Against such a marksman I will not shoot. I did not ween in all England there dwelt such an one save only Robin Hood of Sherwood Forest."

"Now, Robin Hood, Robin Hood, Robin Hood," quoth the Sheriff in hot anger. "Who says to me always Robin Hood? There be plenty of better marksmen than he, and the cowardly knave hath not even dared show his face here in my presence this day! Come hither, fellow." The ragged beggar approached to the foot of the Sheriff's splendid seat. "Here take the prize. Thou hast won it fairly enough," and he handed to him the gold and silver arrow. "Now hark! I bid thee join my service. With me thou shalt be well paid and thou shalt eat and drink of the best. There is no good man in any line but I call to my standard, and since thou hast defeated William O'Leslie, thou must be my man. Marry, I rejoice that thou art a better marksman than that coward Robin Hood, and one day we will show him full fair the worth of the Sheriff of Nottingham's men!"

The beggar looked up with a twinkle in his one sorry eye.

"I will serve thee, O Sheriff, as thou deservest!" said he.

"Here, fellow," the Sheriff turned to a huge lumbering rogue in the uniform of his guards, who appeared suddenly beside the

beggar. "Take this man to the barracks! Henceforth he shall dwell midst the best marksmen in Nottinghamshire."

The eye of the huge fellow twinkled and he gave a prodigious wink. "Aye, aye," says he, "I will take him to the spot where dwell the best marksmen in Nottinghamshire!" And he clamped his huge hand on the beggar's shoulder and led him into the crowd.

At sunset in the depths of Sherwood Forest, Robin Hood emerged amidst much laughter from the tatters of the beggar, while Little John cast off the garments of the soldier.

"Now, now," says Little John. "I have kept my promise and brought thee where dwell the best marksmen in Nottinghamshire."

"Aye," quoth Robin, "but I have still to keep my promise of serving that rascally Sheriff as he hath deserved. I like not that he called Robin a coward for fearing to come to the match!"

That night the Sheriff sat dining in the great hall of his house in Nottingham-town, with gay candles on the long table, sending dancing shadows to play hide and seek over the dishes and down the long rows of men-at-arms who sat below the Sheriff and his lady. All men talked of the shooting.

"By my troth!" cried the Sheriff. "I did not reckon that knave Robin so great a coward as to fear to come to the contest. Let that good fellow who won the prize come hither to me."

But lo! as men looked among the archers at the foot of the table, the prize-winner was nowhere to be seen, nor neither that huge lumbering fellow in the uniform of the guard who had led him from the field. And even as the Sheriff's attendants sought for the two, hiss! a gray goose shaft shot in at the window, just missing the Sheriff's nose and so startling him that he came near tumbling out of his chair. Recovering himself with much dignity, the Sheriff picked up the arrow from among the dishes before him. Tied to it was a little scroll. Unrolling the same, he read:

May heaven bless thy grace this day,
Say all in sweet Sherwood;
For thou didst give the prize away
To merry Robin Hood!

With an angry snarl the Sheriff crushed the scroll in his hand.

II

Now of a moonlight night soon after this Robin Hood and his men sat about in a circle in their greenwood glade, and out from a lodge built of rustic boughs in a fragrant bower on the edge of the wood came the minstrel Allen-a-dale with his fair bride Ellen, whom Robin and his men had saved of late from being by her father wedded perforce to a rich and rascally baron. And Allen and Ellen took their seats on the soft grass in the circle and Allen sang to his silver-toned harp, plaintiff, mournful, sweet old ballads of England. "*There lived a lass in yonder dale, and down in yonder glen, O!*" and many another such. Then rose Robin Hood from the circle and wandered away alone down a moonlit

Farewell to the Forest, by Mendelssohn, and MacDowell's *Woodland Sketches* portray the forest Robin Hood loved.

trail through the wildwood. It was a fairy night of witching elfin splendor; the glistening silver moonbeams went coquetting with the shadows, peeping from a thicket saucily but to flit away on the instant as if in dainty mischief, calling delicately to mind sweet fancies of the Fairy Queen, Titania, and Oberon, the Elfin King, and jolly Robin Goodfellow, and all those other sprightly elfin folk who once danced their merry round within the moonlit greenwood. All the beauty of the night went warm to Robin's heart, but ah! good Robin was lonely. He, too, loved a lassie, a bonny, bonny lassie, yet would he never coax her from her safe and sheltered home to share his wild life in the forest. Thinking on his dear Maid Marian, he strode slowly down the path.

So he came at last to a narrow little bridge over a babbling brook where he had first met Little John and made occasion to challenge him months agone to a contest. There Little John had proved himself so skillful at play of quarter staves as to pitch bold Robin into the brook, wherefore bold Robin had invited him to join his band and ever after dearly loved him. As he stood by this memorable spot, he saw come tripping down the road a jaunty little page with a feather in his cap.

"Now, by my faith," said Robin to himself, "though I see yon fellow none too clearly, his look speaks overmuch of courts and baron's halls to be to my liking. Still he hath broad shoulders and a confident gait. I will e'en try his mettle. He cannot seem more lackadaisical than did Will Scarlet, when first I tested him, yet is no better man in my band. I'll e'en test this youth!" And covering his face with his kerchief, Robin stepped out on the bridge.

"Ho, fellow!" he cried roughly. "Stop and march back whence thou came; for none passes here save as I will; and marry, my jolly good blade can play a right merry tune!"

"Nay now, good sir," quoth the page full courteously. "I mean no mischief, but have business beyond. Pray let me pass."

"Pass thou shalt not, save over my head on my sword's point!"

"Pass then I will," cried the page. "My humor is to do no man harm, yet in sooth my business lieth across this bridge!" And he drew his sword and came forward right sturdily. Now it was a merry sight to see how that sweet youth fell to with his blade, how bold were the strokes he struck, and how stoutly he stood to his own defence. It was click and clack and thwack and whack, and a scratch here for Robin and a scratch there for the page, nor had either one whit the better of the other, till at last good Robin dropped his rough and threatening voice and cried once more in his own fair tone: "Enough, courteous stranger! Put up thy sword. I have tried thee and found thee, in spite of thy clothes, a right sturdy fellow. Come, join my band and range the greenwood with me. 'Tis Robin Hood bids thee!" And he pulled the kerchief from off his face. Then Lauk-a-mercy! The youth dropped his sword and crumpled up in a heap, and all his bold strength vanished and he cried in a weak little voice:

"O Robin, so near had I wounded thee! Dost thou not know thine own Maid Marian? I fled from the scoundrel Sheriff who would force me to wed his cross-eyed son, and here am I come to the greenwood just to seek thee, my Robin, O!"

"Marian! My lassie!" Good Robin could scarce believe his ears and he raised up the maiden and held her face to the moonlight, and there sure enough, but with hair cut short like a boy's, was his own dear lassie. "Marian, mine only dear!"

"Come to dwell with thee, Robin, in the greenwood forever!"

Then Robin's heart leaped like a doe for joy and he took his true-love by the hand and led her back to fair Ellen's bower in the greenwood glade, and fair Ellen received Maid Marian with gladness and gave her shelter for the night. When the morrow was come, Maid Marian and Robin were wedded by Friar Tuck in the great cathedral of the arching wildwood, and lo! what a day it was for joy. For of all merry days in the forest, it was the first of May, the festival of the coming of Spring, when lads and

The gay music of the opera, *Robin Hood*, by Reginald de Koven, makes one feel actually out-of-doors. "Come Away to the Woods" and "A-Hunting We Will Go" have all the merry lilt of Robin's life.

IN SHINING ARMOR

lassies from the villages came out a-maying, and burst from the woodland paths into the greenwood glade, their arms filled with flowers, their heads decked with wreaths and over all the fragrance of the white hawthorn bloom. And they romped singing and laughing about Maid Marian and made her Queen of the May. They set her up high on a throne of green boughs and crowned her with garlands. Then Robin Hood's men cut down the tallest and straightest birch tree in the wood and set it up for a Maypole in the centre of the glade, while the maidens wreathed it about with flowers, and the lads fastened to its top long streamers of gay-colored ribbons with little tinkling bells. When all was done, came merry dancers, some in rag-tags of costumes, some in simple clothes of the countryside, and lads and lassies each seized a ribbon and fell a-dancing—twisting, turning, weaving gracefully, singing a merry song. With quips and sports and pranks the day

The English celebrate May Day by erecting Maypoles on village greens, while dancers weave colored ribbons to and fro as they sing. English folk songs are full of the freshness of spring and dancing on the green.

was filled. There were contests at quarter-staves and wrestling, and Robin Hood's men set up the willow wands hung with garlands that served them for targets, and held a shooting match, the victor being crowned with a wreath by Maid Marian, Queen of the May. A stately feast closed the gladsome day, then lads and lassies went back once more to the little thatched cots in the villages. But Maid Marian was come in sooth to stay in the green-wood, and Robin Hood built for her a lodge in a flowery bower, and there, sharing Robin's life, she continued to dwell.

III

It happened all on a Summer's day that Robin Hood leaned him against a tree and said to Little John: "Today is a fair day, Little John, and I make mine avow that I will not dine till thou hast brought me here some bold baron, knight or squire to be my guest. Take then thy good bow in thine hand and let Much and Will Scarlet wend with thee up to Watling Street to fetch me a guest. See ye do no party any harm that hath a woman in it, nor no husbandman, nor no yeoman, nor no knight nor squire that will be a good fellow, but, purse-proud baron or pompous earl, bring willy-nilly to me. If my guest be over-rich he shall pay for the feast; if poor, I will share my goods with him."

"Marry, good Master," quoth Little John, "Right glad I am to obey." And off he went with Much and Will Scarlet, till through highways and byways they came out at last on that fine old road that was builded in days long gone by the Romans and hight Watling Street. They looked east, they looked west and no man did they see, but by and by came a knight a-riding past, all dreary of semblance and poorly clad.

Little John advanced full courteously and fell upon his knee.

"Welcome to the greenwood, gentle Knight," said he. "My master hath waited fasting these three long hours to dine with thee."

"Who is thy master?" quoth then the Knight.

"My master is Robin Hood."

"Ah, a good yeoman," said the Knight. "Of him I have heard much good and so doth it please me to dine with him."

Yet ever as they went their way, the tears rolled down the good Knight's cheeks, and a sorry man he seemed. Unto Robin Hood's lodge they led him; and there with much good will and manner fair and courteous, did Robin bid him welcome. Then answered the gentle Knight:

"God save thee, good Robin, and all thy fair many. I am called Sir Richard of the Lea, and right gladly will be thy guest."

So the board was laid on the trestles and the cloth was spread. Robin and his guest washed together and wiped together and sat them down to meat with Maid Marian and the rest.

"Such a dinner have I not had in many a year," quoth the Knight, when he had eaten his fill.

"If it hath pleased thee, sir Knight," said Robin Hood, "then I prithee pay for the feast! Surely thou knowest it was never the custom that a yeoman should pay for a knight."

"I take thy meaning," said the Knight gravely, "yet have I naught in my coffers to offer thee."

"Nay now," quoth Robin Hood, "too many of thine order these days keep no troth with Truth. Speak honestly."

"I have no more but ten shillings," said the Knight full sorrowfully, "for sooth as I you say!"

"If that be true," cried Robin, "then I will not have of thee one penny. And if thou have need of any more, more shall I lend thee."

The good Knight opened his purse and shook out ten shillings.

"Alack! the more pity," quoth Robin Hood. "Hast thou then been a poor husbandman and let thy lands go to ruin to fall in so sorry a case?"

"Nay, by my faith," cried Sir Richard. "No such fault is mine. My son, for that there are those who hate him high in favor at court, was cast into prison on a paltry charge, and to get him free I must e'en pay a ransom of four hundred pounds.

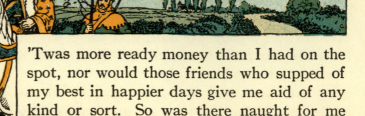

'Twas more ready money than I had on the spot, nor would those friends who supped of my best in happier days give me aid of any kind or sort. So was there naught for me to do but go to the rich Lord of Ely for aid. A wicked hard bargain the baron drove with my need. For the loan of four hundred pounds I must pledge him all my fair lands and castle worth three score times the same, nor would he leave me the money to work my land and earn once more wherewithal to repay him. Now the day of settlement is come and here am I on my way to tell him I cannot pay him a penny. What will he do but seize my castle and lands! O, alack! I grieve not for myself but for my dear wife and tender babes that have nowhere to lay their heads."

Now for ruth of this sad tale wept Maid Marian and Little John and Will Scarlet, and many another stout fellow there. And Maid Marian whispered somewhat in Robin Hood's ear. Then cried Robin Hood loudly: "Sir Richard of the Lea, if no other man be thy friend in need, then is Robin Hood that man." And he rose up from the board. "Little John, go to my treasure and tell me out four hundred pounds. Will Scarlet, measure me three yards each of our stoutest green and scarlet cloth!"

Off went Little John and Will Scarlet, but that large hearted fellow, Little John, made such pretense of stupidity at counting, that for four hundred pounds he told out eight and twenty score, while Will Scarlet boldly measured yards by his good six-foot bow.

"If our measure be over-full," said Little John, "yet what better alms can there be than to help a poor gentle knight that is fallen in poverty?" So they bore all back to Robin, who gave it unto Sir Richard while the good Knight wept for thanks.

"And when shall I come to repay thee?" said he.

"This day twelvemonth," said Robin, "under this trystel tree."

Meantime in the dining hall of Ely Castle, where blue and crimson light from the high arched windows streamed over the richly spread table, sat the baron at meat, and with him, all in splendid robes, his friend, the Lord High Sheriff of Nottingham.

"Now, friend Sheriff," says the baron in the Sheriff's ear, "but an Sir Richard come this very day to pay me, he shall be dispossessed and all his fair lands fall to me. A good bargain I made—to purchase for four hundred pounds an estate that will yield me full four hundred pounds every year. Now, remember, I paid thee thy good fat fee to see that the case proceeds all in fair process of law. I count on thee to uphold me."

"Aye," said the Sheriff. "But I prithee do not forget when betwixt us both Sir Richard is fleeced, that thou owest me still another fat fee, for my services at the shearing!"

Now even as they spoke, Sir Richard was announced and, clad in his poor sorry garments, into the great room he came.

"Do gladly, my lord," says he. "I am come to keep my day."

"Hast thou brought my pay?" cried the baron.

"Not a penny," quoth the Knight; and the baron's eyes sparkled covetously. "Those fair lands are mine!" thought he.

"My lord," Sir Richard said; "I beg thee for longer time."

"Never a single day more! Forfeit thy lands, this hour!"

"Good Sheriff, be thou my friend. Declare my lands may not be forfeit for a paltry four hundred pounds."

"Nay," quoth the Sheriff sternly. "I hold with my Lord of Ely. Thy lands are forfeit this day."

"But my wife and tender babes, where shall they lay their heads?"

"That concerns us not," cried the Sheriff. "Thy wife is *thy* wife. Do thou find where she may lay her head. My lord, what wilt thou give this fellow if he signs the release at once?"

"A hundred pound," said the baron, "and not a penny more."

"Take the hundred pounds, Sir Knight, if thou hast wits," quoth the Sheriff, "and let the matter end."

"Nay, now!" cried the Knight, on a sudden loosing all the bold spirit pent within. "Though ye gave me a thousand pounds, yet would I never sign the release!" He strode to a round table standing hard by, and shook out of a bag that he held in his hand an even four hundred pound. "Have here thy gold, my lord!" he cried, "which that thou lentest me! Hadst thou been courteous at my coming, I should have rewarded thee. But thou hast bespoken me villainously, so shalt thou have not a penny more but thy four hundred pound. Now have I repaid thy loan on the very day and shall have my lands again for aught that thou canst do!" And off he strode, merrily whistling, to tell his fair lady at home how their castle and lands were free.

But that purse-proud baron he left behind had no more stomach for bite or sup, for all his royal fare.

"Give me back my gold that I paid thee in fee to get me these lands," he roared in the Sheriff's ear.

"Never a penny will I give back! Thou shouldst not have brought a fox instead of a sheep to the shearing!" And they fell to at quarrel and squabble, but in such care of their skins as to have nary a weapon that was more sharp than their tongues!

It chanced on a day soon after, that Robin sent Little John, Much, the Miller's son, and Will Scarlet again to Watling Street to bring back a guest for dinner, and whom do they see come ambling down the long white road but a pompous baron, splendidly clad, and that right worshipful Sir, The Lord High Sheriff himself, and with them two and fifty wight young men for guard.

"Now, my Lord of Ely," the Sheriff was saying, "thou doest well to go to London and start proceedings at law against that same fellow, Sir Richard, that of late rode his high horse with thee. I ween thou wilt still find some legal means to strip him of his lands, and in London the name of the Sheriff of Nottingham is well known at court. Thou wilt still find it to thy vantage to have such an one to thy friend."

"Little hast thou vantaged me thus far!" growled the Lord of Ely. But even at that moment, Little John, Much, and Will Scarlet stopped the cavalcade, and said right courteously:

"Worshipful sirs, our master bids thee dine with him."

"Master! Who may thy master be?" quoth the Lord of Ely.

"My master is Robin Hood," saith Little John very gently.

"Robin Hood!" cried the Sheriff. "He is a thief and a robber!"

"Robin Hood!" cried the Lord of Ely. "Of him heard I never good!" and the two started up their horses and bade their young men ride on. Then blew Little John a blast on his silver horn, and all the wood along the road seemed alive with men in Lincoln green, with bows strung and arrows aimed at the cavalcade. Went up a cry from the two and fifty wight young men that guarded the baron and sheriff, and marry! they all turned tail and fled, leaving their masters a-snivelling and cursing fast in Little John's hands. So Little John and his men blindfolded the two and led them off to Robin Hood's lodge.

"Do gladly, right worshipful sirs," says Robin Hood full courteously, "I bid you welcome to dinner!"

"Do gladly, right worshipful sir," stammered the Sheriff. "We thank thee but are not an-hungered!"

Yet was there naught for the Sheriff and baron to do but wash with Robin and wipe with Robin and set themselves down with him to the board, while their knees knocked together for fear. Right sumptuous was the dinner, but little stomach to food had the guests, and when the Sheriff saw at head of the table as Robin's own lady that same bonny lass, Maid Marian, whom, willy-nilly, he had meant to wed to his son, he choked on a bitter mouthful and must e'en be pounded well on the back or ever he found his breath once more. Dinner over and done, quoth Robin in courteous wise, "Now, worshipful sirs, that you have dined of our best, I pray you pay for the feast!"

Whined the Lord of Ely, "But twenty marks have I with me!"

"And naught but two pounds with me," quoth the Sheriff.

"If this be true, good sirs," said Robin, "then will I take from you not one penny, for never I rob no poor man; but if you have lied, then, by my faith, will I take all you have."

And he bade Little John turn out the contents of the two men's saddle bags. Little John spread out his mantle, and from the Lord of Ely's bag poured out chinking eight hundred pounds in gold, "Wherewith he was on his way to start proceedings in London to fleece Sir Richard!" cried Little John. And from the Sheriff's bag rolled two hundred pounds, fee in full wherewith the baron had bribed him to sanction his fleecing Sir Richard.

"Now," quoth Robin. "Here is the quickest payment that ever yet saw I me. Look where in three days is settlement made of Sir Richard's debt to me!" And he took the money and bade Little John lead the howling Lord of Ely back once more to the road. "But thou, Sir Sheriff," says he, "hast so long been our friend that we cannot so quickly part with thee. Thou shalt stay for a twelvemonth with us! An outlaw we'll make of thee!"

"Heaven have mercy," cried the Sheriff. "Let me go, I pray!"

But they took off his satins and velvets and linens and wrapped him in Lincoln green, and there 'neath the greenwood by night he must sleep on the hard, hard ground, and by day dress the King's deer, that the outlaws shot, and scrape vegetables, and wash kettles and pots, and serve as a common scullion. At the end of a fortnight's time a sorrier man than that Sheriff ne'er dwelt by dale or down.

"Ere I lie another night here," cried he, "now, Robin, I pray thee, smite off mine head and I will forgive it thee."

IN SHINING ARMOR

"Ah," laughed bold Robin. "We aim but to teach thee to be a good outlaw."

"Now for Saint Charity," cried the Sheriff, "let me go, and I will be the best friend that ever you had."

"Then," quoth Robin sternly, "by my bright sword thou shalt swear never more to do harm to my men nor me, nor to those poor folk in the countryside whom I make it mine affair to aid."

And that Sheriff he swore him a mighty oath, never more to harm Robin nor his men nor those poor folk of the countryside. Then he took his satins and velvets and home he went, nor journeyed abroad in the greenwood again for many a long day to come.

So the year rolled round; passed the time for gathering the harvest home, when reapers sang 'neath the harvest moon, passed the time of snow-laden forest trees with crackling of fires in the greenwood huts, and roasting of crabs, and ballad and song. Came the springtime once more with singing of birds, and Sir Richard all in fine array to pay his debt 'neath the greenwood tree.

"For that I have my lands once more, thank I God, and thee," quoth he to good Robin. "This year have I prospered, and here have I brought the four hundred pounds to repay thee, and some little gifts of good bows and arrows beside."

But Robin embraced and welcomed him well and told him how that in sound justice he was already repaid on the third day after the borrowing, and that settlement being far and away above the amount of the debt, he gave good Sir Richard thereof four hundred pounds more to build up his lands and once more work them to good advantage. So Robin holp Richard of all his cares and ever they two were fast friends henceforth.

IV

Now when the King in London-town heard all that went forward in Sherwood Forest, how that there a bold outlaw dwelt who killed the King's deer that none but the King might shoot, and defied the officers of the crown and never could be captured,

"By my kingdom," quoth he, "I'll take him myself!" and away with a mighty many he rode to Nottingham-town. But though he scoured the countryside he saw no sign of Robin. Said an old forester then: "Liege, take five of thy men alone, dress thyself as an abbot, thy men as monks. Then roam at large in the greenwood and I'll warrant thou wilt soon fall in with Robin Hood."

The King made no delay at carrying out of the plan. And in sooth he had not gone far when out stepped bold Robin and bade the abbot and his men come with him to dine. Blindfolded, he led them away, in thought to relieve them of any over-abundance of this world's goods. But the King, when he reached the greenwood quoth: "I am a messenger come from the King to bid thee, bold Robin, come to Nottingham to be his guest both at meat and meal."

Then cried Robin, "If such thou art, in sooth not a penny will I take from thee, for I love no man in all the world as I love my good liege lord, that doth ever tilt with barons and clergy to win fair justice for yeomanry! Welcome, thou, to the greenwood!"

"If thou lovest thy liege," said the King, "methinks thou shootest a many of his deer."

"Aye, but," says Robin, "the deer in truth belong to him not—all the game of the forest should be free, free to the people who need it, and not to serve but as sport to him who needs it not. All men have equal rights and if the King's law agree not, then must it give place to the better law of the greenwood."

Now the King said to himself that Robin's words rang true, though never would it do to admit it! So they washed together and wiped together and when they had dined full well Robin summoned his men and they showed their guest what sort of life merry-men led in the greenwood, shooting their arrows at targets placed at six score paces. "Who misseth the mark," cried Robin, "getteth a blow on the head!"

Twice Robin shot and cleft the wand, and so did Gil o' the White Hand, best archer of them all, but Little John's arrow went astray and Will Stutely likewise missed; so Robin bade stout Will Scarlet smite them each a buffet, and such a buffet he smote that they both fell flat to the ground. And at the last shot, what should chance but Robin himself missed the mark by three fingers' width and more.

"Ha! Ha!" laughed Gil o' the White Hand. "Master, thou hast lost. Now like thy men, stand forth and take thy pay."

"So must it be," quoth Robin, shamefaced, "what is good for a man is good for the master, Sir Abbot, I deliver thee mine arrow and since I have failed of my mark, I pray thee smite me well."

"I like not to smite a good yeoman," said the King; but he folded up his sleeve and gave such a buffet to Robin that he sprawled full length on the ground!

"Mine avow to God," quoth Robin, "thou art a stalwart friar!"

As he spoke, the monk's cowl fell back and Robin saw the King's face. Then sudden he fell on his knee.

"My lord, the King!" he cried. And down on their knees fell his men.

"Fear naught from me," quoth Robin, "my men and I crave mercy, my lord and liege, from thee."

"Mercy, good Robin, shalt thou have," cried the King, full heartily. "For well have I seen 'tis sheriffs and such as they that in this day true outlaws be, and here in the heart of the greenwood dwelleth freedom and true justice. Come thou and thy men to my service, for much have I need of stout arms like thine, and stout hearts like thine and true, to do battle with such outlawry as dwelleth in the hearts of the rich and powerful. Come and I pledge thee my word I shall not rest till outlawed Justice find once more her seat in the common courts of the land!"

"I make mine avow to God," says Robin. "Thou speakest nobly. I am right glad to serve so stout a lord." And all the sevenscore men in Lincoln green hurled up their caps in air and shouted too: "We are right glad to serve so stout a lord."

And so it befell, when that the King went back to Nottingham-town, there went Robin likewise, Maid Marian and fair Ellen, and all their goodly company of merry men withal.

"Hast captured the outlaw then?" quoth the Sheriff in glee.

"Nay," the King made answer. "The outlaw hath captured me! And for the love of his hardihood have I made him Captain of my guard. His first duty, Sir Sheriff, shall be to bring thee in chains to London, there to answer to me for the felonies thou hast committed in the name of the law of the land!"

It was a goodly many save for the poor, sorry Sheriff that set off for London-town all on a summer's day.

"Belike our life will be busy in service of the King," quoth Robin in Marian's ear; "yet sometimes we'll slip away and hie us once more to the greenwood on a merry morn in May, to see the deer draw to the dale and hear the small birds sing!"

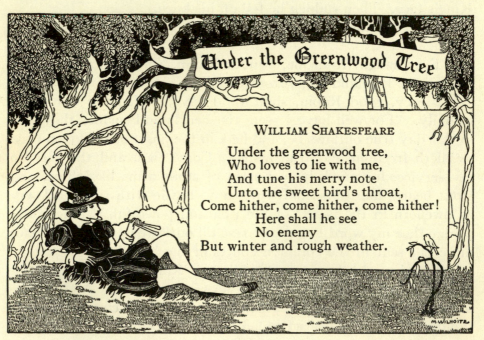

Under the Greenwood Tree

WILLIAM SHAKESPEARE

Under the greenwood tree,
Who loves to lie with me,
And tune his merry note
Unto the sweet bird's throat,
Come hither, come hither, come hither!
Here shall he see
No enemy
But winter and rough weather.

IN SHINING ARMOR
The Tale of the Rhine-Gold
A Germanic Epic retold from the operas of Richard Wagner

Long, long ago, there lay on a rock in the cool green depths of the Rhine, a gleaming hoard of gold. Catching the beams of the sun, it shed them down through the waves to gladden the waterfolk. Such was the natural use of the gold, and for the joy it brought, it was loved and adored by water sprites who swam around it singing. But the Old Man of the Rhine, the ancient River-god, knew that the gold might be seized by someone willing to give up love. It might be forged into a ring, which would give its owner tyrannical power to grind down the weak and helpless and make himself lord of the earth. So the Rhine-god set his daughters, three saucy water-nymphs, to guard the precious gold. Laughing and chasing each other, they played in the emerald waves, singing alluring songs and darting in and out among the jagged rocks.

But now below the Rhine, hidden in mists and darkness, lay Nibelheim, home of the Nibelungs, ugly little dwarfs who dug the metals of earth and forged them with cunning as smiths. One day just before sunrise, while the Rhine went melodiously thundering on its majestic course to the sea, there climbed up through a chasm from misty Nibelheim, the little Nibelung, Alberich. Awkward, clumsy, heavy, slipping on the wet rocks, sneezing, protesting, he came; but seeing now above him three shimmering maiden forms, moving quick and graceful in merry dives and capers, he lost his heart on the instant, fell madly in love with their beauty, and, calling, he begged the Rhine-nymphs to let him join their play.

The old Germanic story of the magic ring is told by one of the greatest German composers, Richard Wagner, in four great operas, *The Rhine-Gold*, *The Valkyrie*, *Siegfried*, and *Twilight of the Gods*.

Startled at first, the three rallied to guard their gold, but seeing in the twilight only a dark little dwarf, they thought him a harmless creature, and forgetting their task of watching, they sought a little amusement by teasing their clumsy wooer. Each in turn flattered him sweetly, inviting him to embrace her and then slipped out of his grasp with maliciously musical laughter just as he thought he had her. "Impudent fish! Deceitful young ladies!" he shrieked; but as he pursued them madly, suddenly he stood still. Blue and phosphorescent, a light appeared in the water. Growing in size and radiance, it turned the waves to light! The sun had risen at last and kindled the fire of the gold! Forgetting their tantalized victim, the naughty Rhine-nymphs began to swim around their idol, singing in wildest joy: "Rhine-gold! Rhine-gold! Luminous joy! How laughest thou so bright and clear!"

"What is it gleaming up there?" Alberich cried in awe; whereon the silly maidens poured out all their secret. "That which gleams is the Rhine-gold. He who casts from him the joys of love can forge that gold into a ring which will make him lord of the earth!"

"All who live wish for love," the foolish maidens thought. "None would give up love and so the treasure is safe!" But thanks to their own naughty pranks, Alberich at that moment was scarcely in love with love! Ambition awoke in his heart! To make the world tremble before him,—the little, ugly Nibelung,—for this he would give up love! With hate-inspired strength, he climbed the rock, while the nymphs in crazy high spirits laughed with foolish glee. Tearing from its socket that splendid light of the waves, he plunged with it into the depths, leaving sudden night in the waters. Shocked into sense, the Rhine-nymphs cried wildly "Help!" and "Woe!" But from the caves of Nibelheim, only Alberich's laugh, harsh, discordant, triumphant, mockingly drifted back.

Meantime, far above in the sky, Valhalla, the newly-built castle of Wotan, King of the gods, towered up story on story, its gleaming spires and pinnacles pricking the very clouds.

Wotan had employed the giants, Fasolt and Fafner to build him this castle and had promised them as reward, Freya, goddess of beauty and youth, who raised the magic apples that kept the gods eternally young. But now that the castle was finished, Fricka, Wotan's wife, cried out in great dismay that they could never give Freya, in payment to the giants.

"Nay," replied Wotan-the-one-eyed; "I meant not to keep my word! Loki promised to find a way whereby I may evade it!"

Now Loki, the mischief-maker, destructive lord of fire, was forever seeking means to get the gods into trouble; for he was but half a god and secretly hated Wotan, whose strong spear had subdued him. Calm and majestic was Wotan, mighty and august, but, alas, he was ambitious, and to build his great Valhalla, he had permitted Loki to tempt him into a bargain he never meant to keep. He, whose powerful spear was the mystic guardian of compacts, had been tempted to injustice, and Loki knew well that there reigned above Wotan in the universe, a Power of absolute righteousness. If Wotan disobeyed this, then Wotan himself must fall!

With colossally heavy tread, and carrying as walking-sticks enormous trunks of trees, the giants came for their pay. Good Fasolt, shaggy and blonde, in tunic of snow-white fur, loved the beautiful Freya with all his big, soft heart, but Fafner, dark-browed and evil, wanted only riches and power.

Plainly Wotan announced that he would not give them Freya, whereon the burly creatures seized the maid for themselves. Just then, high up on the rocks, like a darting tongue of flame, Loki, the vivid and charming, clad all in scarlet, appeared, and he announced that Alberich had forged of the Rhine-gold a ring which could make its owner lord of the earth. "Get us that ring, O Wotan, and we will accept it in payment in place of Freya!" cried Fafner; and though Fasolt objected strongly to giving up the maid, it was at last agreed that if Wotan paid them the ring and the treasure of the Nibelungs, Freya should at nightfall be returned to the gods.

Down through a sulphur-cleft to the caves of Nibelheim, Loki now guided Wotan. Thick vapors poured from the cleft, a dull red glow tinged the vapor, and as they went further down the sounds of tiny hammers beating on tiny anvils, fell upon their ears. They had come to the world of the Nibelungs, the little toiling smiths. Here by the power of his ring, Alberich now reigned, savage, hateful, cruel, darkened by love of gold, and tyrannical love of power. He entered the gloomy cave driving before him with his scourge, a miserable, huddling throng of little smoke-begrimed Nibelungs, groaning under the weight of great pieces of gold and silver which he had made them forge, while Meemy, his little gnome-brother, forever ground down by his blows, cowered in fear in a corner, having just been soundly beaten because he was slow in forging a magic wishing cap. Perceiving the lordly Wotan with his self-sufficient calm, Alberich, drunk with power, began a wild boasting and raving, and so eager was he to show off for the august King of the Gods, that Loki easily tricked him. Begging him to show them the power of the magic cap, Loki made Alberich turn himself into a little toad, whereupon Wotan immediately set his foot upon him, and as Loki snatched off the cap, there in his own shape was Alberich writhing and squirming piteously under Wotan's boot. Easily the gods bound him and bore him to upper-earth, and there while Loki went dancing

mockingly around him, snapping his fingers and leaping as heart-lessly merry as fire, Wotan forced him to give up, first, all his hoard of gold, which the Nibelungs brought from the earth, and after that, the ring. Beside himself with rage, Alberich uttered a curse on all who should own that ring. "Let it mean death to the wearer! Let him be gnawed by envy, jealousy, and care!"

And now when the giants at nightfall returned with the lovely Freya, Fasolt, still loving the maid, declared that if he took gold in her stead, they must pile the treasure so high he could no longer see her. Therefore, at Wotan's command, attendants heaped up the treasures around the blooming maid. "More gold! More gold! More!" Fafner greedily cried. "I can still see the shining of her hair!" And when all the gold was gone, Fasolt insisted: "But look, I can still see the gleam of her eyes!" So to stop up that last cranny, Fafner demanded the ring. But by this time, Wotan himself coveted the ring; he would not give it up, till shedding a weird bluish light, out of the earth there rose the upper half of a woman, and Erda, the dark earth-spirit, as one awakened from sleep, cried aloud to Wotan: "Avoid the curse of the ring. The present order passeth! I see the end of the gods!" So saying, she sank back to earth, while Wotan deeply moved, flung the ring on the pile. Thus satisfied at last, the giants gave back Freya, and began to pack up their gold; but at once they fell to quarreling over which one should have the ring, and Fafner, raising his tree-trunk, struck his brother dead, then walked off with all the gold, while the gods stood appalled to see how quickly the curse had worked. And now through the mists of the valley there beat a terrific storm,

Wagner's first opera of the "Ring" series, *The Rhine-Gold*, tells the story thus far. Given in almost total darkness, it is gloomy with the mocking laughter of dwarfs, the moaning of water-nymphs, and the overshadowing curse.

which clearing before the sunlight, showed vaulting way up to Valhalla, tremulous, tender, gorgeous, the shimmering Bridge of the Rainbow, over which the gods ascended to their home.

The end of the gods was to come, the earth-spirit had foretold it! To prepare for that final struggle Wotan gathered from earth an army of human heroes, sending eight of his daughters, the wild and war-like Valkyrs, to hover over battle-fields and carry the slain to Valhalla, on their fiery steeds of the air.

If Alberich were to recover the ring, how powerful to fight the gods he would be in that last day! Fafner, the evil giant, absorbed by love of the gold, had turned himself into a dragon by means of the magic cap, and in a forest-girt cave, he guarded his precious hoard; but to get the ring for himself now became Wotan's great aim. He could not seek it directly since he had given it to Fafner in just repayment of a debt; but he planned a round-about way to gain the end he sought. Descending to earth, he made himself into a mortal called Wolf, and, clad in a shaggy wolf-skin, he took a human wife. Then in a hut in the woods were born to him sturdy twins, Siegmund, a little lad, and Sieglinda, a pretty maid. This Siegmund, Wotan meant should recover for him the ring, and since it was law that gave the right of the ring to Fafner, he brought the boy up with wild courage and disregard for the gods, knowing no higher law than the law of his own big heart. But when Siegmund was still very young, Wotan took him out hunting and while they were gone, their foe Hunding, burned their hut to the ground, slew the beloved mother, and carried off the little maid. What sorrow of heart for Siegmund! Apart from woman's sweet influence, he grew up alone with Wotan, until his father, too, vanished, leaving only his wolf-skin behind. And then with no other companion, Siegmund grew to manhood, a noble but tragic youth, the sweet impulses of his heart, the kindliness of his soul, keeping him ever at variance with the oft-times cruel laws of men. One day he defended a maid, whose kindred, fulfilling their rights,

IN SHINING ARMOR

were trying to force the girl to wed a man she despised. Fighting till the girl was slain and all his weapons gone, Siegmund burst staggering and panting into the nearest house, a primitive wooden dwelling built round a huge oak tree. As he lay on the ground half-swooning, a woman lovely and gracious, mercifully came to his aid. And now, though he knew it not, this dwelling belonged to Hunding and she who waited upon him was Sieglinda, his long-lost sister, whom the ugly and hated Hunding had forced to be his wife. When Hunding returned from the fight, he having been of the kindred that slew the unfortunate maid, he was wroth to see in his house the protector of the maiden. Moreover, he soon suspected that Siegmund was a Volsung, the son of Wolf, his foe. So though he ate with the hero, and, true to hospitality's laws, refrained from attacking a guest, he cried that on the morrow, Siegmund must leave his house and meet him in hostile fight.

In the long, dark hours of the night Siegmund alone and weaponless longed for a good, stout sword to fight that next day's battle, then in the soft rays of moonlight he saw the lovely Sieg-

linda come gently into the room and gently steal up to his side. Pointing out a sword which stuck to its hilt in the tree that grew up through the center of the hall, she told him that a one-eyed stranger had put it there on her wedding day, declaring that none save he for whom the gods intended it, would be able to draw it forth. Many a man, said Sieglinda, had vainly tried to remove it; Hunding himself had tried; but now let Siegmund attempt it. For him might be the sword!

Eagerly advancing, Siegmund seized the hilt, and giving a vigorous pull, he drew the sword from the tree, for so had Wotan in secret provided a sword for his son. "*Nothung*, or Sword-in-need shall be the name of this sword," Siegmund exultingly cried, and his famished heart was filled with such overflowing love for the beautiful woman who helped him, that he clasped her close to his breast and begged her to fly with him from her hateful husband, Hunding, out from the shadows and gloom into the glory of moonlight, and the laughing house of the Spring! Rapturously Sieglinda yielded to his wooing. How happy they two could be, to whom the hearts' full joy had been so long denied! They knew not they were brother and sister, but hand in hand as lovers they stole out into the world. And when Hunding on the morrow found Sieglinda vanished, he set out in furious rage to punish the guilty pair.

Wotan's son was in danger! The King of Gods called Brunhilda, best-loved of his Valkyrie daughters, and bade her watch over the battle, giving Siegmund the victory. But now across the sky in her chariot drawn by rams, Fricka, his wife came to him, the law-abiding *Hausfrau*, and forcefully she reminded him that Siegmund had broken laws by defending a maid from her kindred, then by taking off Hunding's wife, who was in fact his own sister; and Wotan whose spear stood irrevocably for the sanctity of the law could not give the victory to one who broke the law! Bitterly Wotan recognized the truth of what she said. Calling Brunhilda to him, he reversed his first command, gave up the hopes of years, and bade her give victory to Hunding. In spite of her wild, eager pleadings, he insisted that this must be done.

Sadly Brunhilda went to warn the bold young hero, and finding him in the woods with Sieglinda's head in his lap, she bade him prepare for Valhalla. But Siegmund boldly said if Sieglinda might not go with him, he would not go to Valhalla! And the warrior-maid of the skies was so moved by the depth of his love, that she disobeyed her father and protected Siegmund in the fight.

IN SHINING ARMOR

In the midst of thunder and lightning, Wotan himself appeared
and broke Siegmund's sword with his spear. Then Hunding struck
Siegmund dead, only to fall himself before the withering scorn of
Wotan's scorching glance. Brunhilda seizing Sieglinda and the
bits of Siegmund's sword, fled in haste on her air-horse, while
Wotan, riding the storm-wind, followed in hot pursuit. To the high
plateau where the Valkyrs came like a thundering charge of horsemen, bearing the bodies of heroes, Brunhilda fled for refuge. Sieglinda, with *Nothung*, the Sword, she sent to the woods alone just as
Wotan arrived in his wrath. For her disobedience, he condemned
Brunhilda to be no more a goddess, no more a battle-maiden, but a
mere spinning mortal woman. On that plateau she must sleep to
be the bride of any man who should chance to come and awake
her. All her tears and pleadings could only wring from her father
the promise that she should be guarded by a barrier of living flames,
so that only the bravest of heroes would ever break through and
claim her. Holding the glorious maid close, Wotan kissed her eyes
into sleep. He laid her on the ground, and struck the rock with
his spear. Flickering flames shot forth, rising ever higher, roaring,
crackling, leaping, forming a wall of fire to guard the sleeping maid.*

*Wagner's opera, *The Valkyrie*, ends here. The wild "Ride of the Valkyrie," with their shouts and the neigh-
ing of their steeds is tremendous and the fire music, as the flames leap forth swelling ever brighter, is thrilling.

Meantime in direst need, Sieglinda wandered alone in the depths of primeval forest, till she came to the cave of Meemy, Alberich's little dwarf-brother. Here she gave birth to Siegmund's son, the lusty infant Siegfried. Then dying, she entrusted to Meemy her babe and the broken sword. So in the grand old forest a second hardy Volsung, Siegfried, grew to manhood, knowing nothing of his parentage save that the wily Meemy pretended he was his son. Joyous, big, and strong, simple, sane, and fearless, the youth soon felt contempt for the cringing little dwarf, whose protests of affection he knew to be mere pretence.

While Siegfried ranged the forest on friendly terms with the beasts, climbing the tallest trees and scaling the steepest rocks, Meemy dreamed that this fearless youth should some day get him the ring by slaying the terrible Fafner, and he tried to forge him a sword; but the best sword he could forge, the strong young Siegfried could break. Holding a bear in leash and frightening poor little Meemy so he scurried all over the cave, Siegfried one day came home bursting with youthful strength. Who were his mother and father? He would no longer accept Meemy's affectations and lies! He wanted to know about love. Rough young cub that he was, he longed to know about love! He had seen how the birds paired, built nests, and raised their little ones. He had seen the deer, the foxes, and wolves,—how the father brought food to the lair and the mother nursed the young. He had learned from them what love was and he had never robbed the mother of her young. But Meemy knew no such love! Meemy could not be his father! With youthful, insistent violence he forced from Meemy the truth. Beautiful, sad Sieglinda, glorious but tragic Siegmund,—these were his mother and father, and there lay the broken bits of *Nothung*, his father's sword! Bidding Meemy forge him a weapon from those shining, heroic bits, Siegfried rushed from the cave.

But now while Meemy labored, Wotan came to see him. Since Fricka had made him see that the maker of laws must be governed by his own laws, he could no longer hope to get the ring for himself. He saw that his own dishonesty in dealing with the giants and stealing the cursed ring, had set evil forces in motion, which had grown till he could not govern them, and would finally overwhelm him; yet Siegfried was his grandson, and he was still interested in who should get the ring. Throwing Meemy into a panic he told him that only one who knew not the meaning of fear should forge the sword and slay Fafner; but that same one who knew no fear would be the slayer of Meemy! What could Meemy do now? If he kept Siegfried free from fear, he might slay Fafner perhaps, but he would also slay Meemy! If Meemy valued his life, he must make Siegfried feel that fear was to be desired. So when Siegfried burst in again, crying: "Hey, there, lazy-bones, have you finished the sword?" Meemy began to ask him if he had never known the delightful sensation of fear. In the dark woods at twilight, with weird and mysterious sounds of rustling, sighing and muttering and will-o'-the-wisps a-flickering,—had Siegfried never then felt a shuddering in his limbs, a trembling and wild beating heart? Meemy quaked at the thought; but Siegfried, simple and childlike, cried in amusement and wonder:

"I long to know that delight, that creeping and that shuddering, but, alas! my heart stands ever firm and serene in its place!"

So Meemy told Siegfried he knew where dwelt Fafner, a terrible dragon, who could surely teach Siegfried to fear. Loudly demanding his sword, Siegfried declared he would go with pleasure to meet this dragon and learn that delightful sensation; but finding that Meemy had even yet failed to forge his father's sword, he angrily seized the pieces, heaped the fuel on the hearth, and began to forge it himself, singing a lusty song: "Hoho! Hoho! Hahei! Hahei! Blow, bellows, brighten the glow! *Nothung*, notable sword!"

Meantime Meemy, half-crazed with fear that Siegfried would one day slay him, secretly brewed a poison to kill the youth in his victory, and then he led him forth to wait before Fafner's cave. In the beauty of the summer's day, with delicate shafts of sunlight piercing the wavering leaves and playing on the forest floor, the lonely boy's heart dwelled longingly on the thought of his mother and father, and he tried to imagine in fancy how they must have looked. But across the glow of his dreams cut the vivid warble of a bird. If he could only understand the language of the birds! Cutting a reed, he made a pipe and tried to imitate with the merry notes of his piping the beautiful song of the bird. "If I sing his language!" he cried, "I shall perhaps understand him!" But all this was in vain. He could not understand the bird. So he threw away his pipe and blew a gay call on his horn, trying what that would do. This produced no effect on the bird but it roused fearful Fafner from sleep and out of his cavern he came, a frightful, fire-breathing dragon, bellowing and roaring. The sight roused no fear in Siegfried; it only made him laugh. "Ha, ha!" he cried. "My lure hath charmed forth something lovely!" A terrible struggle ensued, with the dragon's yawning jaws and spouting breath of flame, threatening terrific destruction; but still Siegfried knew no fear; he calmly waited the moment when he could plunge his sword clean through the dragon's heart. Then Fafner's enormous coils relaxed in the stillness of death. Siegfried drew forth his sword and licked from his finger a drop of the venomous dragon's blood. Suddenly he noted that thus he had been made able to understand the speech of birds.

"Enter the cave! There is treasure there! Take the helmet and ring!" a little bird plainly said. So Siegfried entered the cave and took the helmet and ring; but the treasure meant nothing to him. He loved neither gold nor power, and he left the hoard there in the dark. As he came out again in the light, he found little Meemy and Alberich quarreling over the question as to who was to have the ring, but the little bird warned him now to be on his guard against Meemy. So when the mean little dwarf offered him refreshment in the shape of a poisoned drink, he slew him with one stout blow, and while Alberich laughed in glee over the death of his brother, Siegfried flung the carcass of Fafner to guard the door of the cave, and putting the whole matter from him, he turned to leave the spot. But now what said the bird? He sang of a beautiful maiden asleep up there on the mountain surrounded by a wall of fire and to be won as a bride only by the man who knew not the meaning of fear. How charming that sounded to Siegfried! Love, that was what charmed him, not the lure of gold, not the lust of power, the tender warmth of love, the glow of sweet affection! He followed the lead of the bird up, up the mountain-side. Wotan appeared to test him, to see if he knew no fear; but Siegfried raised his sword and shivered Wotan's spear and steadily kept on his way. Before him he saw the fire, the leaping sheet of flame. But into that furnace he leapt, singing his merry hunting-song or blowing a wild-wood note from the silvery tones of his horn. As he boldly faced the flames, lo, they sank before him and he saw a figure in armor asleep on the fresh green grass! A man he thought it to be and he took off the shield and helmet, he cut through the thongs of the breast-plate, but, lo, to his surprise, he saw rippling out in the sun-light a flood of golden hair, shimmering in glory. This was no man but a maiden, and as he fell by her side, he felt his heart beat so fast and his limbs so deliciously tremble that he thought at last he knew fear! With a kiss he awakened the maiden and love glowed warm in their hearts.

IN SHINING ARMOR

Then Brunhilda grieved no more to give up the state of a goddess, but rejoiced to be only a woman and to the young hero, a wife.*

For years in joy and happiness they two dwelt together in love up there on the mountain-top with a wall of fire to guard them. But the time came at length when Siegfried must go forth into the world to do a man's deeds again; and giving Brunhilda the ring as a pledge of his undying love, he bade her a tender farewell.

Now by this time, the miserable Alberich had an evil son, Hagen, whom he meant to use as a tool to get back the cursed ring, and knowing that Siegfried would probably soon arrive at Worms, Hagen advised his half-brother, the weak but resplendent Prince Gunther, to take to wife Brunhilda, and since Gunther dared not pierce through the wall of flames to win her, to bid their sister Gutrune give Siegfried a magic drink which should make him love her so madly, he would promise to win her hand by securing Brunhilda for Gunther. Neither Gunther nor Gutrune knew Brunhilda was Siegfried's wife, and so they agreed to the plan. Merrily blowing his horn, Siegfried arrived in a boat, all his power and gaiety displayed in the easy stroke with which he guided the craft. But no sooner had pretty Gutrune given him Hagen's draught, than alas, for the joy of his life! he quite forgot Brunhilda, and, madly in love with Gutrune, agreed to Gunther's plan. Using the magic cap, he gave himself Gunther's shape and piercing the wall of flames, overcame Brunhilda's resistance and brought her back to Gunther. And now what grief and surprise, what incomprehensible sorrow for the faithful and loving Brunhilda!

*Wagner's opera, *Siegfried*, continues the story to this point. *Siegfried*, in contrast to the other operas, is light and joyous, full of the happiness of youth and love, and alive with the impetuous vitality of the hero.

A wedding feast she saw, and Siegfried, disdaining her utterly, declaring he did not know her, determined to wed Gutrune and denying the pledge of the ring!

In a moment of wild Valkyrian wrath, Brunhilda agreed that Hagen should kill her inconstant husband. She told him that she herself had secretly by her charms rendered all Siegfried's body impenetrable to wounds save a single spot on his back. Next day when the men went to hunt, and sat at the hunting feast, Hagen gave Siegfried a draught which restored his memory; but in the very moment when Siegfried recalled Brunhilda and lovingly called her name, Hagen stabbed him in the back.

While men bore the dead hero home on his shield, Hagen sought Gutrune, who anxiously awaited her beloved lord's return. Brutally he announced that Siegfried had been slain. Wild was Gutrune's grief; but Brunhilda, now knowing the truth, her heart again warm to Siegfried, bade men make a funeral pyre, a mighty pyre worthy a hero. Then, joyously mounting her steed, she uttered her jubilant Valkyr's cry and plunged boldly into the flames! Let the Rhine-nymphs come and reclaim their ring from the mingled ashes of the lovers! Love was stronger than death! Love could deliver the earth from the terrible curse of the ring, such was Brunhilda's last cry! Wildly the flames sprang up burning the palace of Gunther, reaching the very skies and firing the great Valhalla. In one immense conflagration, lit from the pyre of the lovers, earth and heaven blazed and the old gods passed away, the gods who had been unjust. They passed to make room for the reign of a greater and holier power, the reign of righteousness, truth and justice among men. And as the flames receded, the thundering Rhine arose, and the Rhine-nymphs riding the waves to the funeral pyre of Siegfried, seized the precious ring. Hagen, in wild despair, reaching to snatch it from them, was pulled in the water and drowned; while the nymphs, with cries of triumph, bore the gold back to the Rhine, to be no more a ring, giving men tyrannical power to enslave the weak and helpless, but a joy to the water-folk, a shining light to the waves.

Wagner's opera, *Twilight of the Gods*, ends his "Ring" series. No other composer ever wrote such tremendous music. Today a Wagner festival is regularly held at Bayreuth, where these operas were first presented in 1876. See Vol. V, page 179.

The Surprising Adventures of
Don Quixote of La Mancha
MIGUEL DE CERVANTES
Edited by Frances Jenkins Olcott

THERE once lived, in a certain village of La Mancha in Spain, a gentleman who did apply himself wholly to the reading of old books of knighthood. And that with such gusts and delights, as he neglected the exercise of hunting; yea and the very administration of his household affairs.

He plunged himself so deeply in his reading of these books that he spent in the lecture of them whole days and nights. And in the end, through his little sleep and much reading, he dried up his brains in such sort as he lost wholly his judgment.

His fantasy was filled with those things that he read, of enchantments, quarrels, battles, challenges, wounds, wooings, loves, tempests, and other impossible follies. And these toys did so firmly possess his imagination that the dreamed inventions which he read were true, that he accounted no history in the world to be so certain and sincere as they were.

Finally, his wit being wholly extinguished, he fell into one of the strangest conceits; to wit, it seemed unto him very needful, as well for his honour, as for the benefit of mankind, that he himself should become a knight-errant, and go throughout the world, with his horse and armour, to seek adventure, and practice in person all that he had read was done by knights of yore, revenging of all kinds of injuries, and offering himself to dangers, which once happily achieved, might gain him eternal renown.

He resolved to give himself a name worthy of so great a knight as himself, and in that thought he laboured eight days; and in conclusion called himself Don Quixote of La Mancha. Then he donned certain old armour that had belonged to his great-grandfather, mounted his old lean horse, Roz'i-nan'te, and sallied forth into the world to seek adventure.

Don Quixote by the Austrian composer, Richard Strauss, born in 1864, portrays in a series of tone pictures Don Quixote, Sancho Panza, the battle with the sheep, the meeting with Dulcinea, and other incidents of this story

IN SHINING ARMOR

With him rode as his squire, one San'cho Pan'za, a labourer, and an honest man, but one of very shallow wit. Don Quixote had said so much to him, had persuaded him so earnestly, and had made him so large promises, that the poor fellow determined to go away with the knight, and serve him as his squire. Don Quixote bade him to dispose himself willingly, for now and then such an adventure might present itself, that in as short space as one would take up a couple of straws, an island might be won, and Sancho be left as governor thereof.

This same squire, Sancho Panza, did ride upon an ass. About the ass Don Quixote had stood a while pensive, calling to mind whether ever he had read that any knight-errant carried his squire assishly mounted; but he could not remember any authority for it. Yet, notwithstanding, he had resolved that Sancho might bring his beast, intending to dismount the first discourteous knight they met from his horse, and give it to his squire.

Don Quixote bethought himself that now he wanted nothing but a lady on whom he might bestow his service, and affection. For a knight-errant that is loveless resembles a tree that wants leaves and fruit, or a body without a soul. He bethought him of a damsel who dwelt in the next village to his manor, a young handsome wench with whom he had been some time in love, although she never knew or took notice thereof. Her he chose as the Lady of his thoughts, she being ignorant of it, and he called her Dul-cin'e-a of To-bo'so.

Things being thus ordered, Don Quixote and his squire rode forth into the world, and had, with some good success, many ridiculous and rare adventures, as well as some that were dreadful and never-imagined—all worthy to be recorded. All these adventures may be read in that strange book, The History of the Valorous and Witty Knight-Errant, Don Quixote of La Mancha.

Herein will be related three of his adventures, to wit: The Dreadful and Never-Imagined Adventure of the Windmills; How

Don Quixote Fought with Two Armies of Sheep and The High Adventure and Rich Winning of the Helmet of Mam-bri'no.

THE DREADFUL AND NEVER-IM-AGINED ADVEN-TURE OF THE WINDMILLS

THE first day that Don Quixote and his squire, Sancho Panza, sallied forth to seek adventure, they travelled almost all day without encountering anything worthy the recital, which made Don Quixote fret for anger. For he desired to encounter presently some one upon whom he might make trial of his invincible strength. Riding thus, toward evening they discovered some thirty or forty windmills, that were in a field. And as soon as Don Quixote espied them he said to his squire:

"Fortune doth address our affairs better than we ourselves could desire. For behold there, friend Sancho Panza, how there appear thirty or forty monstrous giants, with whom I mean to fight, and deprive them of their lives, with whose spoils we will begin to be rich. For this is a good war, and a great service unto God, to take away so bad a seed from the face of the earth."

"What giants?" quoth Sancho Panza.

"Those that thou seest there," quoth his lord, "with the long arms. And some there are of that race whose arms are almost two leagues long."

"I pray you understand," quoth Sancho Panza, "that those which appear there are no giants, but windmills. And that

which seems in them to be arms, are their sails, that, swung about by the wind, do also make the mill go."

"It seems well," quoth Don Quixote, "that thou art not yet acquainted with the matter of adventures. They are giants. And, if thou beest afraid, go aside and pray, whilst I enter into cruel and unequal battle with them."

And, saying so, he spurred his horse Rozinante, without taking heed to his squire Sancho's cries, who called out that they were windmills that he did assault and no giants. But Don Quixote went so fully persuaded that they were giants that he neither heard his squire's outcries, nor did discern what the windmills really were, although he drew very near to them.

Then he called out to them as loud as he could:

"Fly not, ye cowards and vile creatures! for it is only one knight that assaults you."

With this the wind increased, and the mill sails began to turn about; which Don Quixote espying, said:

"Although thou movest more arms than the giant Briareus, yet thou shalt stoop to me."

And, after saying this, desiring Lady Dulcinea to succour him, he covered himself well with his buckler, and set his lance on his rest. Then he spurred on Rozinante and encountered with the first mill that was before him. As he struck his lance into the sail, the wind swung it about with such fury, that it broke his lance into shivers, carrying him and his horse after it, and finally tumbling him a good way off from it on the field in very evil plight.

Sancho Panza repaired presently to succour him as fast as his ass could drive. And when he arrived, he found his lord not able to stir, he had gotten such a crush with Rozinante.

"By my beard!" quoth Sancho, "did I not foretell unto you that you should look well what you did, for they were none other than windmills? Nor could any think otherwise, unless he had also windmills in his brains."

"Peace, Sancho," quoth Don Quixote; "for matters of war are more subject than any other thing to continual change; how much more, seeing that some magician—such is the enmity he bears towards me—hath transformed these giants into mills to deprive me of the glory of the victory. But yet, in fine all his bad arts shall but little prevail against the goodness of my sword."

"God grant it as He may!" said Sancho Panza, and then he helped his master arise; and presently he mounted him on Rozinante, who was half shoulder-pitched by the rough encounter. And thus discoursing upon the adventure they followed on the way which guided towards a passage through the mountains. For there, as Don Quixote avouched, it was not possible but to find many adventures because it was a thoroughfare much frequented.

HOW DON QUIXOTE FOUGHT TWO ARMIES
OF SHEEP

ONE day Don Quixote and his squire while they rode, perceived a great and thick dust to arise in the way wherein they travelled. Turning to Sancho, Don Quixote said: "This is, Sancho, the day wherein shall be manifest the good which fortune hath reserved for me. This is the day wherein the force of mine arm must be shown as much as in any other whatsoever; and in it I will do such feats as shall forever remain recorded in the books of fame. Dost thou see, Sancho, the dust which ariseth there? Know that it is caused by a mighty army and sundry and innumerable nations, which come marching there."

"If that be so," quoth Sancho, "then must there be two armies; for on this other side is raised as great a dust."

Don Quixote turned back to behold it, and seeing it was so indeed, he was marvellous glad, thinking that they were doubtless two armies, which came to fight one with another in the midst of that spacious plain.

The dust which he had seen, however, was raised by two great flocks of sheep, that came through the same field by two differ-

ent ways, and could not be discerned, by reason of the dust, until they were very near. Yet Don Quixote did affirm that they were two armies so earnestly that Sancho believed it, and demanded of him: "Sir, what then shall we two do?"

"What shall we do," quoth Don Quixote, "but assist the needful and weaker side? For thou shalt know, Sancho, that he who comes towards us is the great Emperor A-li-fam'fa-ron, lord of the great island of Trap-o-ban'a; the other, who marcheth at our back, is his enemy, the King of the Gar'a-man'tes, Pen-tap'o-lin of the naked arm, so called because he still entereth in battle with his right arm naked."

"I pray you, good sir," quoth Sancho, "to tell me why these two Princes hate one another so much?"

"They are enemies," replied Don Quixote, "because that this

Alifamfaron is a furious pagan, and is enamoured of Pentapolin's daughter, who is a very beautiful and gracious Princess. Her father refuseth to give her to the pagan King, until first he abandon Mahomet's false sect, and become a Christian Knight."

"By my beard," quoth Sancho, "Pentapolin hath reason, and I will help him all that I may."

"By doing so," quoth Don Quixote, "thou performest thy duty; for one need not be a knight to enter into such battles."

"I do know that myself," quoth Sancho, "very well; but where shall we leave this ass in the meantime, that we may be sure to find him again after the conflict?—For I think it is not the custom to enter into battle mounted on such a beast."

"It is true," quoth Don Quixote; "that which thou mayest do is to leave him to his adventures, and care not whether he be lost or found; for we shall have so many horses, after coming out of this battle victors, that very Rozinante himself is in danger to be changed for another. But be attentive; for I mean to describe unto thee the principal knights of both the armies; and to the end thou mayest the better see and note all things, let us retire ourselves over there to that little hillock, from whence both armies may very easily be descried."

They did so; and, standing on the top of a hill, from whence they might have seen both the flocks, Don Quixote, seeing in fancy that which he really did not see at all, began to say, with a loud voice:

"That knight which thou seest there with the yellow armour, who bears in his shield a lion, crowned, crouching at a damsel's feet, is the valorous Laurcalio, lord of the silver bridge. The other, limbed like a giant, that standeth at his right hand, is the undaunted Brandabarbaray of Boliche, lord of the three Arabias, and comes armed with a serpent's skin, bearing for his shield, as is reported, one of the gates of the temple which Samson overthrew.

"But turn thine eyes to this other side, and thou shalt see first of all, and in the front of this other army, the ever victor and never vanquished Ti'mo-nel of Car-ca-jo'na, Prince of New Biscay, who comes armed with arms parted into blue, green, white, and yellow quarters, and bears in his shield, in a field of tawny, a cat of gold, with a letter that says Miau, which is the beginning of his lady's name, which is, as the report runs, the peerless Mi-ai-lin'a, daughter of Duke Alfeniquen of Algarve."

And thus Don Quixote proceeded forward, naming many knights of the one and the other squadron, even as he had imagined them. And he attributed to each knight his arms, his colours, and mottoes, for he was suddenly borne away by the imagination of his wonderful distraction.

Sancho Panza stood suspended at his master's speech, and spoke not a word, but only would now and then turn his head, to see whether he could mark those knights and giants which his lord had named; and, by reason he could not discover any, he said:

"Sir, I give to the devil any man, giant, or knight, of all those you said did appear; at least I cannot discern them. Perhaps all is but enchantment, like that of the ghosts of yester-night."

"How sayst thou so?" quoth Don Quixote. "Dost not thou hear the horses neigh, the trumpets sound, and the noise of the drums?"

"I hear nothing else," said Sancho, "but the great bleating of many sheep."

And so it was, indeed; for by this time the two flocks did approach them very near.

"The fear that thou conceivest, Sancho," quoth Don Quixote, "makest thee that thou canst neither hear nor see aright; for one of the effects of fear is to trouble the senses, and make things appear otherwise than they are. And, seeing thou fearest so much, retire thyself out of the way; for I alone am sufficient to give the victory to that army which I shall assist."

And, having ended his speech, he set spurs to Rozinante, and, setting his lance in the rest, he flung down from the hillock like a thunderbolt.

Sancho cried to him as loud as he could, saying: "Return, good sir Don Quixote! for I vow unto God, that all those which you go to charge are but sheep and muttons; return, I say. Alas, that ever I was born! what madness is this? Look; for there is neither giant, nor knight, nor cats, nor arms, nor shields parted nor whole, nor pure azures nor devilish. What is it you do? Wretch that I am!"

For all this Don Quixote did not return, but rather rode, saying with a loud voice, "On, on, knights! all you that serve and march under the banners of the valorous Emperor Penta-polin of the naked arm; follow me, all of you, and you shall see how easily I will revenge him on his enemy, Alifamfaron of Trapobana."

And saying so, he entered into the midst of the flock of sheep, and began to lance them with such courage and fury as if he did in good earnest encounter his mortal enemies.

The shepherds that came with the flock cried to him to leave off; but, seeing their words took no effect, they unloosed their slings, and began to salute his pate with stones as great as one's fist. But Don Quixote made no account of their stones, and did fling up and down among the sheep, saying:

"Where art thou, proud Alifamfaron? Where art thou? Come to me; for I am but one knight alone, who desires to prove my force with thee man to man, and deprive thee of thy life, in pain of the wrong thou dost to the valiant Pentapolin."

At that instant a stone gave him such a blow on one of his sides, as did bury two of his ribs in his body. He beholding himself so ill dight, did presently believe that he was either slain

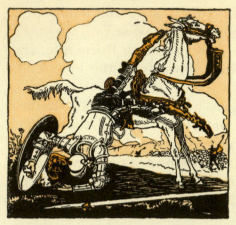

or sorely wounded. And, remembering himself of his oil-pot, which he thought to contain some magic healing liquor, set it to his mouth to drink. But ere he could take as much as he thought requisite to cure his hurts, there cometh another stone, which struck him so full upon the hand and oil-pot, as it broke it into pieces, and carried away with it besides three or four of his cheek teeth, and did moreover bruise two of his fingers.

Such was the first and the second blow, as the poor knight was constrained to fall down off his horse. And the shepherds arriving, did verily believe they had slain him; and therefore, gathering their flocks together with all speed, and carrying away their dead muttons, which were more than seven, they went away without verifying the matter any further.

Sancho remained all this while on the height, beholding his master's follies, pulling the hairs of his beard for very despair; and he cursed the hour and the moment wherein he first knew him. But seeing him overthrown to the earth, and the shepherds fled away, he came down to him, and found him in very bad plight, yet had the knight not quite lost the use of his senses.

"Sir Knight," quoth Sancho, "did not I bid you return, and tell you that you went not to invade an army of men, but a flock of sheep?"

"That thief, the magician who is mine adversary," quoth Don Quixote, "can counterfeit and make men to seem such, or vanish away, as he pleaseth; for, Sancho, thou oughtest to know that it is a very easy thing for men of that kind to make us seem what they please; and this magician that persecuteth me, envying the glory which he saw I was like to acquire in this battle, hath converted the enemy's squadrons into sheep. If thou wilt not believe me, Sancho, yet do one thing for my sake, that thou mayest remove thine error, and perceive the truth which I affirm. Ride ahead on thine ass, and follow the armies fair and softly aloof, and then thou shalt see that, as soon as they are parted any distance from hence, they will turn to their first form, and, leaving to be sheep, will become men, as right and straight as I painted to thee at first. But go not now, for I have need of thy help and assistance. I pray thee, give me thy hand, and feel how many cheek teeth, or others, I lack in this right side of the upper jaw."

Sancho put in his finger, and whilst he felt him, demanded, "How many cheek teeth were you accustomed to have on this side?"

"Four," quoth he, "besides the hindermost; all of them very whole and sound."

"See well what you say, sir," quoth Sancho.

"I say four," quoth Don Quixote, "if they were not five; for I never in my life drew or lost any tooth."

"Well, then," quoth Sancho, "you have in this lower part but two teeth and a half; and in the upper neither a half, nor any; for all there is as plain as the palm of my hand."

"Unfortunate I!" quoth Don Quixote, hearing the sorrowful news that his squire told him, "for I had rather lose one of my arms, so it were not that of my sword; for, Sancho, thou must know, that a mouth without cheek teeth is like a mill without a mill-stone; and a tooth is much more to be esteemed than a diamond. But we knights-errant which profess the rigorous laws of arms are subject to all these disasters; wherefore, give the way, gentle friend; for I will follow thee what pace thou pleasest."

Talking thus they rode on their way where they thought they might find lodging, and about nightfall they perceived an inn near unto the highway wherein they travelled, which was as welcome a sight to Don Quixote as if he had seen a star that did guide him to the porch, if not to the palace, of his redemption.

THE HIGH ADVENTURE OF THE HELMET OF MAMBRINO

THE next morning as Don Quixote and his squire were riding over the plains it began to rain, and Sancho would fain have sought shelter in some near-by mill, but Don Quixote would in no wise come near one. But, turning his way on the right hand, he fell into a highway, as much beaten as that wherein they rode the day before. Within a while after, he espied one a-horseback, that bore on his head something that glistered like gold. And scarce had he seen him, when he turned to Sancho, and said:

"Methinks, Sancho, that there's no proverb that is not true; for they are all sentences taken out of experience itself, which is the universal mother of sciences; and especially that proverb that says: 'Where one door is shut another is opened.' I say this because, if fortune did shut yesterday the door that we searched, deceiving us in the adventure of the armies, it lays for us now wide open the door that may lead us to a better and more certain adventure, whereon, if I cannot make a good entry, the fall shall be mine. If I be not deceived, there comes one towards us that wears on his head the helmet of Mam-bri'no, which I have made an oath to win."

"See well what you say, sir, and better what you do," quoth Sancho; "for I would not wish that this were new shepherds to batter you."

"The devil take thee for a man!" replied Don Quixote; "what difference is there betwixt a helmet and shepherds?"

"I know not," quoth Sancho, "but if I could speak as much now as I was wont, perhaps I would give you such reasons as you yourself should see how much you are deceived in that you speak."

"How may I be deceived in that I say, scrupulous traitor?" demanded Don Quixote. "Tell me, seest thou not the knight which comes riding towards us on a dapple-grey horse, with a helmet of gold on his head?"

"That which I see and find out to be so," answered Sancho, "is none other than a man on a grey ass like mine own, and brings on his head something that shines."

"Why, that is Mambrino's helmet," quoth Don Quixote. "Stand aside, and leave me alone with him. Thou shalt see how, without speech to cut off delays, I will conclude this adventure, and remain with the helmet as mine own which I have so much desired."

"I will have care to stand off. But I turn again to say, that I pray God that it be a purchase of gold, and not flocks of sheep."

"I have already said unto thee not to make any more mention, no, not in thought, of sheep. For if thou dost," said Don Quixote, "I vow, I say no more, that I will batter thy soul."

Here Sancho, fearing lest his master would accomplish the vow which he had thrown out as round as a bowl, held his peace.

This, therefore is the truth of the history of the helmet, horse and knight, which Don Quixote saw. There were near this spot two villages, the one so little as it had neither shop nor barber, but the greater was furnished with one. This barber did therefore serve the little village when they had any occasion, as it now befell. For which reason he came bringing with him a brazen basin.

And as he travelled, it by chance began to rain, so he clapped his basin on his head to save his hat from staining, because it belike was a new one. And the basin being clean scoured, glistered half a league off.

He rode on a grey ass, as Sancho said, which Don Quixote mistook for a dapple-grey steed, and the barber for a knight, and the basin for a helmet of gold. For Don Quixote did, with all his facility, apply everything which he saw to his raving chivalry and ill-errant thoughts. And when he saw that the poor barber drew near, without settling himself to talk with him, he

inrested his javelin low on the thigh, and ran with all the force Rozinante might, thinking to strike him through and through. And, drawing near unto him, without stopping his horse, he cried:

"Defend thyself, caitiff! or else render unto me willingly that which is my due by all reason."

The barber, who without fearing or surmising any such thing, saw that knight come suddenly upon him, had no other remedy, to avoid the blow of the lance, but to fall off his ass to the ground. And scarce had he touched the earth, when rising up again as light as a deer, he ran away so swiftly through the plain as the wind could scarce overtake him, leaving his basin behind on the ground.

Don Quixote rested content, and commanded Sancho to take up the helmet; who lifting it, said: "The basin is a good one."

Then he gave it to his lord, who presently set it on his head, turning it about every way to see whether he could get the beaver. And seeing he could not find it, he said:

"The pagan for whom this famous helmet was first forged had doubtlessly a very great head. And that which grieves me most is that this helmet lacks the beaver."

When Sancho heard him call the basin a helmet, he could not contain his laughter; but presently remembering his master's anger, he checked himself in the midst.

"Why dost thou laugh, Sancho?" demanded Don Quixote.

"I laugh," said he, "to think on the great head the pagan owner of this helmet had; for it is for all the world like a barber's basin."

"Know, Sancho," quoth Don Quixote, "that this enchanted helmet did fall, by some strange accident, into some one's hands that knew not the worth thereof, who seeing it was of pure gold, without realizing what he did, melted the half, to profit himself therewithal. Then he made of the other half this, which seems a barber's basin, as thou sayest. But be it what it list, to me who knows well what it is, its change makes no matter, for I will dress it in the first town where I shall find a smith. And in the meanwhile I will wear it as I may, for something is better than nothing; seeing it may defend me from the blow of a stone."

"That's true," quoth Sancho, "if the stone be not thrown out of a sling, such as that of the battle of the two armies, when they blessed your worship's cheek teeth, and broke the bottle wherein you carried the most blessed healing potion."

"I do not much care for the loss of it, Sancho," quoth Don Quixote; "for as thou knowest, I have the recipe in memory."

"So have I likewise," quoth Sancho,—bethinking him of the night he had been made ill by it, "but if ever I make it or taste it again in my life, I pray God that here may be mine end. And

more, I never mean to thrust myself into any occasion wherein I should have need of it. For I mean, with all my five senses, to keep myself from hurting any, or being hurt.

"But, leaving this apart, what shall we do with this dapple-grey steed, that looks so like a grey ass? This beast which that barber whom you overthrew left behind? For I think the man is minded not to come back for him again, since he laid feet on the dust and made haste. But, by my beard, the grey beast is a good one!"

"I am not accustomed," quoth Don Quixote, "to ransack and spoil those whom I overcome. Nor is it the practice of chivalry to take their horses and let them go afoot; unless it befall the victor to lose in the conflict his own; for in such a case it is lawful to take that of the vanquished as won in fair war. So, Sancho, leave that horse, or ass, or what else thou pleasest to call it; when his owner sees us departed, he will return for it."

"Truly," said Sancho, "the laws of knighthood are strait, since they extend not themselves to license the exchange of one ass for another. And I would know whether they permit at least to exchange the one harness for another?"

"In that I am not very sure," quoth Don Quixote; "and as a case of doubt (until I be better informed) I say that thou exchange them, if by chance thy need be extreme."

"So extreme," quoth Sancho, "that if they were for mine own very person, I could not need them more."

And presently, enabled by his master's license, he made the change, and set forth his beast with the harness of the barber's ass.

This being done, they broke their fast, and drank from a near-by stream. And, having by their repast cut away all melancholy, they followed on the way which Rozinante pleased to lead them, who was the depository of his master's will, and also of the ass's, who followed him always wheresoever he went, in good amity and company. Thus they returned to the highway, wherein they travelled at random, seeking new adventures.

IN SHINING ARMOR

Wolfert Webber, or Golden Dreams

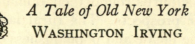

A Tale of Old New York
WASHINGTON IRVING

N THE year of grace one thousand seven hundred and blank, for I do not remember the precise date; however, it was somewhere in the early part of last century, there lived in the ancient city of the Manhattoes a worthy burgher, Wolfert Webber by name. He was descended from old Cobus Webber of the Brill in Holland, one of the original settlers, famous for introducing the cultivation of cabbages, and who came over to the province during the protectorship of Oloffe Van Kortlandt, otherwise called the Dreamer.

The field in which Cobus Webber first planted himself and his cabbages had remained ever since in the family, who continued in the same line of husbandry, with that praiseworthy perseverance for which our Dutch burghers are noted. The whole family genius, during several generations, was devoted to the study and development of this one noble vegetable; and had the portraits of this line of tranquil potentates been taken, they would have presented a row of heads marvellously resembling in shape and magnitude the vegetables over which they reigned.

The seat of government continued unchanged in the family mansion:—a Dutch-built house, with a front, or rather gable end of yellow brick, tapering to a point, with the customary iron weather-cock at the top. Everything about the building bore the air of long-settled ease and security. Flights of martins peopled the little coops nailed against its walls, and swallows built their nests under the eaves. In a bright sunny morning in early summer, it was delectable to hear their cheerful notes, as they sported about in the pure sweet air, chirping forth, as it were, the greatness and prosperity of the Webbers.

Thus quietly and comfortably did this excellent family vegetate under the shade of a mighty button-wood tree. The city gradually spread its suburbs round their domain. Houses sprang up to interrupt their prospects. The rural lanes in the vicinity began to grow into the bustle and populousness of streets; in short, with all the habits of rustic life they began to find themselves the inhabitants of a city. Still, however, they maintained their hereditary character, and hereditary possessions, with all the tenacity of petty German princes in the midst of the empire. Wolfert was the last of the line, and succeeded to the patriarchal bench at the door, under the family tree, and swayed the sceptre of his fathers, a kind of rural potentate in the midst of the metropolis.

To share the cares and sweets of sovereignty, he had taken unto himself a helpmate, one of those notable little housewives who are always busy where there is nothing to do. Her activity, however, took one particular direction: her whole life seemed devoted to intense knitting; whether at home or abroad, walking or sitting, her needles were continually in motion. This worthy couple were blessed with one daughter, who was brought up with great tenderness and care; uncommon pains had been taken with her education, so that she could stitch in every variety of way; make all kinds of pickles and preserves, and mark her own name on a sampler. The influence of her taste was seen also in the family garden, where the ornamental began to mingle with the useful; whole rows of fiery marigolds and splendid hollyhocks bordered the cabbage-beds; and gigantic sunflowers lolled their broad jolly faces over the fences.

Thus reigned and vegetated Wolfert Webber over his paternal acres, peacefully and contentedly. Not but that, like all other sovereigns, he had his occasional cares and vexations. The growth of his native city sometimes caused him annoyance. His little territory gradually became hemmed in by streets and houses, which intercepted air and sunshine. The expenses of living doubled and trebled; but he could not double and treble the mag-

nitude of his cabbages; and the number of competitors prevented the increase of price; thus, therefore, while every one around him grew richer, Wolfert grew poorer, and he could not, for the life of him, perceive how the evil was to be remedied.

This growing care, which increased from day to day, had its gradual effect upon our worthy burgher; insomuch, that it at length implanted two or three wrinkles in his brow; things unknown before in the family of the Webbers.

Perhaps even this would not have materially disturbed the serenity of his mind, had he had only himself and his wife to care for; but there was his daughter gradually growing to maturity. How her blue eyes grew deeper and deeper, and her cherry lips redder and redder! Ah, well-a-day! could I but show her as she was then, tricked out on a Sunday morning, in the hereditary finery of the old Dutch clothes-press, of which her mother had confided to her the key. The wedding-dress of her grandmother, modernized for use, with sundry ornaments, handed down as heirlooms in the family. Her pale brown hair smoothed with buttermilk in flat waving lines on each side of her fair forehead, the chain of yellow virgin gold, that encircled her neck. Suffice it to say, Amy had attained her seventeenth year.

At this critical period a new visitor began to make his appearance under the roof of Wolfert Webber. This was Dirk Waldron, the only son of a poor widow, a fresh gamesome youth. This youngster gradually became an intimate visitor of the family. He talked little, but he sat long. He filled the father's pipe when it was empty, gathered up the mother's knitting-needle, or ball of worsted when it fell to the ground; stroked the sleek coat of the tortoise-shell cat, and replenished the tea-pot for the daughter from the bright copper kettle that sang before the fire. All these quiet little offices may seem of trifling import; but they were not lost upon the Webber family. The winning youngster found marvellous favor in the eyes of the mother, and if the sly glances of the daughter might be rightly read, as she sat bridling and dimpling, and sewing by her mother's side, she was not a whit behind Dame Webber in good-will.

Here arose new cares for poor Wolfert. He was a kind father, but he was a prudent man. The young man was a lively, stirring lad; but then he had neither money nor land. Wolfert's ideas all ran in one channel; and he saw no alternative in case of a marriage but to portion off the young couple with a corner of his cabbage-garden, the whole of which was barely sufficient for the support of his family.

Like a prudent father, therefore, he forbade the youngster the house; though sorely did it go against his fatherly heart, and many a silent tear did it cause in the bright eye of his daughter.

She showed herself, however, a pattern of filial piety and obedience. She never pouted and sulked. On the contrary she acquiesced like an obedient daughter, shut the street-door in her lover's face, and if ever she did grant him an interview, it was either out of the kitchen-window, or over the garden-fence.

Wolfert was deeply cogitating these matters in his mind, and his brow wrinkled with unusual care, as he wended his way on Saturday afternoon to the rural inn, about two miles from the city. It was a favorite resort of the Dutch part of the community, from being always held by a Dutch line of landlords, and retaining an air and relish of the good old times. It was a Dutch-built house, that had probably been a country seat of some opulent burgher in the early time of the settlement. It stood near a point of land called Corlear's Hook, which stretches out into the Sound. The venerable and somewhat crazy mansion was distinguished from afar by a grove of elms and sycamores that seemed to wave a hospitable invitation, while a few weeping willows, with their dank, drooping foliage, resembling falling waters, gave an idea of coolness, that rendered it an attractive spot during the heat of summer.

Here, therefore, as I said, resorted many of the old inhabitants of the Manhattoes, where, while some played at shuffleboard and quoits and ninepins, others smoked a deliberate pipe, and talked over public affairs.

It was on a blustering autumnal afternoon that Wolfert made his visit to the inn. The grove of elms and willows was stripped of its leaves, which whirled in rustling eddies about the fields. The ninepin alley was deserted, for the premature chilliness of the day had driven the company within doors. As it was Saturday afternoon, the habitual club was in session, composed principally of regular Dutch burghers, though mingled occasionally with persons of various character and country, as is natural in a place of such motley population.

Beside the fireplace, in a huge leather-bottomed armchair, sat

the dictator of this little world, the venerable Rem, or, as it was pronounced, Ramm Rapelye. He was a man of Walloon race, and illustrious for the antiquity of his line; his great-grandmother having been the first white child born in the province. But he was still more illustrious for his wealth and dignity; he had long filled the noble office of alderman, and was a man to whom the governor himself took off his hat. He had maintained possession of the leather-bottomed chair from time immemorial; and had gradually waxed in bulk as he sat in his seat of government, until in the course of years he filled its whole magnitude.

"This will be a rough night for the money-diggers," said mine host, as a gust of wind howled round the house.

"What! are they at their works again?" said an English half-pay captain, with one eye, who was a very frequent attendant at the inn.

"Aye, are they," said the landlord, "and well may they be. They've had luck of late. They say a great pot of money has been dug up in the fields, just behind Stuyvesant's orchard. Folks think it must have been buried there in old times, by Peter Stuyvesant, the Dutch governor."

"Fudge!" said the one-eyed man of war.

"Well, you may believe it or not, as you please," said mine host, somewhat nettled; "but everybody knows that the old governor buried a great deal of his money at the time of the Dutch troubles, when the English red-coats seized on the province. They say, too, the old gentleman walks; aye, and in the very same dress that he wears in the picture that hangs up in the family house."

"Fudge!" said the half-pay officer.

"Fudge, if you please!—But didn't Corney Van Zandt see him at midnight, stalking about in the meadow with his wooden leg, and a drawn sword in his hand, that flashed like fire? And what can he be walking for, but because people have been troubling the place where he buried his money in old times?"

Here the landlord was interrupted by several gutteral sounds from Ramm Rapelye, betokening that he was laboring with the unusual production of an idea. As he was too great a man to be slighted by a prudent publican, mine host respectfully paused until he should deliver himself. The corpulent frame of this mighty burgher now gave all the symptoms of a volcanic mountain on the point of an eruption. First, there was a certain heaving of the abdomen, not unlike an earthquake; then was emitted a cloud of tobacco-smoke from that crater, his mouth; then there was a kind of rattle in the throat; at length his voice forced its way into a slow, but absolute tone of a man who feels the weight of his purse, if not of his ideas; every portion of his speech being marked by a testy puff of tobacco-smoke.

"Who talks of old Peter Stuyvesant's walking?—puff—Have people no respect for persons?—puff—puff—Peter Stuyvesant knew better what to do with his money than to bury it—puff—I know the Stuyvesant family—puff —every one of them—puff—not a more respectable family in the province—puff—puff —old standers—puff—Don't talk to me of Peter Stuyvesant's walking—puff—puff—puff!"

Here the redoubtable Ramm redoubled his smoking with such vehemence, that the cloudy volume soon wreathed round his head, as the smoke envelops the awful summit of Mount Aetna.

A general silence followed the sudden rebuke of this very rich man. The subject, however, was too interesting to be readily abandoned. The conversation soon broke forth again from the lips of Peechy Prauw Van Hook. Peechy, who could at any time tell as many stories in an evening as his hearers could digest in a month, now resumed the conversation, by affirming that, to his knowledge, money had, at different times, been digged up in various parts of the island. The lucky persons who had discovered them had always dreamt of them three times beforehand, and what was worthy of remark, those treasures had never been found but by some descendant of the good old Dutch families, which clearly proved that they had been buried by Dutchmen in the olden time.

"Fiddlestick with your Dutchmen!" cried the half-pay officer. "The Dutch had nothing to do with them. They were all buried by Kidd the pirate, and his crew."

Here a key-note was touched that roused the whole company. The name of Captain Kidd was like a talisman in those times, and was associated with a thousand marvellous stories.

The half-pay officer took the lead. He was a man of great weight among the peaceable members of the club, by reason of his warlike character and gunpowder tales. All his golden stories of Kidd, however, and of the booty he had buried, were obstinately rivalled by the tales of Peechy Prauw, who rather than suffer his Dutch progenitors to be eclipsed by a foreign freebooter, enriched every field and shore in the neighborhood with the hidden wealth of Peter Stuyvesant and his contemporaries.

Not a word of this conversation was lost upon Wolfert Webber. He returned pensively home, full of magnificent ideas. The soil of his native island seemed to be turned into gold dust; and every field to teem with treasure. His head almost reeled at the thought;

how often he must have heedlessly rambled over places where countless sums lay, scarcely covered by the turf beneath his feet. His mind was in an uproar with this whirl of new ideas. As he came in sight of the venerable mansion of his forefathers, and the little realm where the Webbers had so long, and so contentedly flourished, his gorge rose at the narrowness of his destiny.

"Unlucky Wolfert!" exclaimed he; "others can go to bed and dream themselves into whole mines of wealth; they have but to seize a spade in the morning, and turn up doubloons like potatoes; but thou must dream of hardships, and rise to poverty—must dig the field from year's end to year's end, and yet raise nothing but cabbages!"

Wolfert Webber went to bed with a heavy heart; and it was long before the golden visions that disturbed his brain permitted him to sink into repose. The same visions, however, extended into his sleeping thoughts, and assumed a more definite form. He dreamt that he had discovered an immense treasure in the centre of his garden. At every stroke of the spade he laid bare a golden ingot; diamond crosses sparkled out of the dust; bags of money turned up their bellies, corpulent with pieces-of-eight, or venerable doubloons; and chests, wedged close with moidores, ducats, and pistareens, yawned before his ravished eyes, and vomited forth their glittering contents.

Wolfert awoke a poorer man than ever. He had no heart to go about his daily concerns, which appeared so paltry and profitless; but sat all day long in the chimney-corner, picturing to himself ingots and heaps of gold in the fire. The next night his dream was repeated. There was something very singular in this repetition. He passed another day of reverie, and though it was cleaning-day, and the house, as usual in Dutch households, completely topsy-turvey, yet he sat unmoved amidst the general uproar.

The third night he went to bed with a palpitating heart. He put on his red night-cap wrongside outwards, for good luck.

Again the golden dream was repeated, and again he saw his garden teeming with ingots and money-bags.

Wolfert rose the next morning in complete bewilderment. A dream, three times repeated, was never known to lie; and if so, his fortune was made. In his agitation he put on his waistcoat with the hind part before, and this was a corroboration of good luck. He no longer doubted that a huge store of money lay buried somewhere in his cabbage-field, coyly waiting to be sought for; and he repined at having so long been scratching about the surface of the soil instead of digging to the centre.

He took his seat at the breakfast-table full of these speculations; asked his daughter to put a lump of gold into his tea, and on handing his wife a plate of slapjacks, begged her to help herself to a doubloon.

His grand care now was how to secure this immense treasure without its being known. Instead of his working regularly in his grounds in the daytime, he now stole from his bed at night, and with spade and pickaxe went to work to rip up and dig about his paternal acres, from one end to the other. In a little time the whole garden, which had presented such a goodly and regular appearance, with its phalanx of cabbages, like a vegetable army in battle array, was reduced to a scene of devastation; while the relentless Wolfert, with night-cap on head, and lantern and spade in hand, stalked through the slaughtered ranks, the destroying angel of his own vegetable world.

Every morning bore testimony to the ravages of the preceding night in cabbages of all ages and conditions, from the tender sprout to the full-grown head, piteously rooted from their quiet beds like worthless weeds, and left to wither in the sunshine. In vain Wolfert's wife remonstrated; in vain his darling daughter wept over the destruction of some favorite marigold. "Thou shalt have gold of another sort," he would cry, chucking her under the chin; "thou shalt have a string of crooked ducats for thy

wedding necklace, my child." His family began really to fear
that the poor man's wits were diseased. He muttered in his sleep
at night about mines of wealth, about pearls and diamonds, and
bars of gold. In the daytime he was moody and abstracted, and
walked about as if in a trance. Dame Webber held frequent
councils with all the old women of the neighborhood, not omitting
the parish dominie; scarce an hour in the day but a knot of them
might be seen wagging their white caps together round her door,
while the poor woman made some piteous recital.

In the meantime Wolfert went on digging and digging; but
the field was extensive, and as his dream had indicated no precise
spot, he had to dig at random. The winter set in before one-tenth
of the scene of promise had been explored. The ground became
frozen hard, and the nights too cold for the labors of the spade.

No sooner, however, did the returning warmth of spring
loosen the soil, and the small frogs begin to pipe in the meadows,
but Wolfert resumed his labors with renovated zeal. Still, however,
the hours of industry were reversed. Instead of working cheerily
all day, planting and setting out his vegetables, he remained
thoughtfully idle, until the shades of night summoned him to his
secret labors. In this way he continued to dig from night to night,
and week to week, and month to month, but not a stiver did he
find. On the contrary, the more he digged, the poorer he grew.
The rich soil of his garden was digged away, and the sand and
gravel from beneath was thrown to the surface, until the whole
field presented an aspect of sandy barrenness.

In the meantime, the seasons gradually rolled on. The little
frogs which had piped in the meadows in early spring, croaked

as bull-frogs during the summer heats, and then sank into silence. The peach-tree budded, blossomed, and bore its fruit. The swallows and martins came, twitted about the roof, built their nests, reared their young, held their congress along the eaves, and then winged their flight in search of another spring; and finally the leaves of the button-wood tree turned yellow, then brown, then rustled one by one to the ground, and whirling about in little eddies of wind and dust, whispered that winter was at hand.

Wolfert gradually woke from his dream of wealth as the year declined. He had reared no crop for the supply of his household during the sterility of winter. The season was long and severe, and for the first time the family was really straitened in its comforts. By degrees a revulsion of thought took place in Wolfert's mind. The idea gradually stole upon him that he should come to want. Haggard care gathered about his brow; he went about with a money-seeking air, his eyes bent downwards into the dust. He could not even pass the city almshouse without giving it a rueful glance, as if destined to be his future abode.

The strangeness of his conduct and of his looks occasioned much speculation and remark. For a long time he was suspected of being crazy; and then everybody pitied him; and at length it began to be suspected that he was poor, and then everybody avoided him. Thus everybody deserted the Webber mansion, everybody but honest Dirk Waldron, who indeed seemed to wax more affectionate as the fortunes of his mistress were in the wane.

Many months had elapsed since Wolfert had frequented his old resort, the rural inn. He was taking a long lonely walk one Saturday afternoon, musing over his wants and disappointments, when his feet took instinctively their wonted direction, and on awaking out of a reverie, he found himself before the door of the inn.

Wolfert found several of the old frequenters of the inn at their usual posts, and seated in their usual places; but one was missing, the great Ramm Rapelye, who for many years had filled the leather-bottomed chair of state. His place was supplied by a stranger, who seemed, however, completely at home in the chair and the tavern. He was rather under size, but deep-chested, square and muscular. His broad shoulders, double joints, and bow knees, gave tokens of prodigious strength. His face was dark and weatherbeaten; a deep scar, as if from the slash of a cutlass, had almost divided his nose, and made a gash in his upper lip, through which his teeth shone like a bull-dog's. A mop of iron-gray hair gave a grisly finish to this hard-favored visage. He wore an old hat edged with tarnished lace, and cocked in martial style, on one side of his head; a rusty blue military coat with brass buttons, and a wide pair of short petti-coat trousers, or rather breeches, for they were gathered up at the knees. He ordered everybody about him with an authoritative air; talking in a brattling voice, that sounded like the crackling of thorns under a pot; damned the landlord and servants with perfect impunity, and was waited upon with greater obsequious-ness than had ever been shown to the mighty Ramm himself.

Wolfert's curiosity was awakened to know who and what was this stranger who had thus usurped absolute sway in this ancient domain. Peechy Prauw took him aside, into a remote corner of the hall, and there, in an under voice, and with great caution, imparted to him all that he knew on the subject. The inn had been aroused several months before, on a dark stormy night, by repeated long shouts, that seemed like the howlings of a wolf. They came from the water-side, and at length were distinguished to be hailing the house in the sea-faring manner, "House-a-hoy!" The landlord turned out with his head waiter, tapster, hostler, and errand-boy—that is to say, with his old negro Cuff. On approaching the place whence the voice proceeded, they found this amphibious-looking personage at the water's edge, quite alone, and seated on a great oaken sea-chest. How he came there, whether he had been set on shore from some boat, or had

floated to land on his chest, nobody could tell, for he did not seem disposed to answer questions; and there was something in his looks and manners that put a stop to all questioning. Suffice it to say, he took possession of a corner-room of the inn, to which his chest was removed with great difficulty. Here he had remained ever since, keeping about the inn and its vicinity. Sometimes, it is true, he disappeared for one, two, or three days at a time, going and returning without giving any notice or account of his movements. He always appeared to have plenty of money, though often of very strange outlandish coinage; and he regularly paid his bill every evening before turning in.

He had fitted up his room to his own fancy, having slung a hammock from the ceiling instead of a bed, and decorated the walls with rusty pistols and cutlasses of foreign workmanship. A greater part of his time was passed in this room, seated by the window, which commanded a wide view of the Sound, a short old-fashioned pipe in his mouth, a glass of rum-toddy at his elbow, and a pocket-telescope in his hand, with which he reconnoitered every boat that moved upon the water.

All this might have passed without much notice, for in those times the province was so much the resort of adventurers of all characters and climes, that any oddity in dress or behavior attracted but small attention. In a little while, however, this strange sea-monster, thus strangely cast upon dry land, began to encroach upon the long-established customs and customers of the place and to interfere in a dictatorial manner in the affairs of the ninepin alley and the bar-room, until in the end he usurped an absolute command over the whole inn. It was all in vain to attempt to withstand his authority. He was not exactly quarrelsome, but boisterous and peremptory, like one accustomed to tyrannize on a quarterdeck; and there was a dare-devil air about everything he said and did, that inspired wariness in all bystanders. Even the half-pay officer, so long the hero of the club, was soon silenced by him; and the burghers stared with wonder at seeing their inflammable man of war so readily and quietly extinguished.

And then the tales that he would tell were enough to make a peaceable man's hair stand on end. There was not a sea-fight, nor marauding, nor freebooting adventure that had happened within the last twenty years, but he seemed perfectly versed in it. He delighted to talk of the exploits of the buccaneers in the West Indies, and on the Spanish Main. How his eyes would glisten as he described the waylaying of treasure-ships, the desperate fights, yard-arm and yard-arm—broadside and broadside—the boarding and capturing huge Spanish galleons! All with what chuckling relish would he describe the descent upon some rich Spanish colony; the rifling of a church; the sacking of a Convent— this would be told with infinite glee, as if he considered it an excellent joke; and then he would give such a tyrannical leer in the face of his next neighbor, that the poor man would be fain to laugh out of sheer faintheartedness. If any one, however, pretended to contradict him in any of his stories, he was on fire in an instant. His very cocked hat assumed a momentary fierceness, and seemed to resent the contradiction, and he would at the same time let slip a broadside of thundering oaths and tremendous sea-phrases, such as had never been heard before within those peaceful walls.

Indeed, the worthy burghers began to surmise that he knew more of those stories than mere hearsay. Day after day their conjectures concerning him grew more and more wild and fearful. The strangeness of his arrival, the strangeness of his manners, the mystery that surrounded him, all made him something incomprehensible in their eyes. He was a kind of monster of the deep to them—he was a merman—he was a behemoth—he was a leviathan—in short, they knew not what he was.

The domineering spirit of this boisterous sea-urchin at length grew quite intolerable. He was no respecter of persons; he contradicted the richest burghers without hesitation; he took possession of the sacred elbow-chair, which, time out of mind, had been the seat of sovereignty of the illustrious Ramm Rapelye. Nay, he even went so far, in one of his rough jocular moods, as to slap that mighty burgher on the back, and wink in his face, a thing scarcely to be believed. From this time Ramm Rapelye appeared no more at the inn; and his example was followed by several of the most eminent customers. The landlord was almost in despair; but he knew not how to get rid of this sea-monster and his sea-chest. Such was the account whispered cautiously in Wolfert's ear by Peechy Prauw as he held him by a button in the corner of the hall, casting a wary glance now and then towards the door of the bar-room, lest he should be overheard by the terrible hero of his tale. Wolfert took his seat in a remote part of the room in silence; impressed with profound awe of this unknown.

The stranger was on this evening in a more than usually communicative mood, and was narrating a number of astounding stories of plunderings and burnings on the high seas. He dwelt upon them with peculiar relish, heightening the frightful particulars in proportion to their effect on his peaceful audience. The honest burghers cast fearful glances at the deep scar slashed across the visage of the stranger, and moved their chairs a little farther off.

The half-pay officer now tried to match the gunpowder tales of the stranger by others equally tremendous. Kidd, as usual, was his hero. The seaman had always evinced a settled pique against the one-eyed warrior. On this occasion he listened with peculiar impatience. He sat with one arm akimbo, the other elbow on the table, the hand holding on to the small pipe he was pettishly puffing; his legs crossed; drumming with one foot on the ground, and casting every now and then the side-glance of a basilisk at the prosing captain. At length the latter spoke of Kidd's having ascended the Hudson with some of his crew to land his plunder in secrecy.

"Kidd up the Hudson!" burst forth the seaman, with a tremendous oath.—"Kidd never was up the Hudson! The Devil's Dans Kammer in your teeth! What the plague do you know of Kidd?"

The half-pay officer was silenced; but Peechy Prauw, who never could remain silent, observed that the gentleman certainly was in the right. Kidd never did bury money up the Hudson, nor indeed in any of those parts, though many affirmed such to be the fact. It was Bradish and others of the buccaneers who had buried money; some said in Turtle Bay, others on Long Island, others in the neighborhood of Hell-gate. "Indeed," added he, "I recollect an adventure of Sam, the negro fisherman, many years ago, which some think had something to do with the buccaneers.

"Upon a dark night many years ago, as Black Sam was returning from fishing in Hell-gate"—

Here the story was nipped in the bud by a sudden movement from the unknown, who laying his iron fist on the table, knuckles

downward, with a quiet force that indented the very boards, and looking grimly over his shoulder, with the grin of an angry bear,—"Heark'ee, neighbor," said he, with significant nodding of the head, "you'd better let the buccaneers and their money alone,—they're not for old men and old women to meddle with. They fought hard for their money; they gave body and soul for it; and wherever it lies buried, depend upon it, he must have a tug with the devil who gets it!"

This sudden explosion was succeeded by a blank silence throughout the room. Peechy Prauw shrunk within himself, and even the one-eyed officer turned pale. Wolfert, who from a dark corner of the room had listened with intense eagerness to all this talk about buried treasure, looked with mingled awe and reverence at this bold buccaneer; for such he really suspected him to be. There was a clinking of gold and a sparkling of jewels in all his stories about the Spanish Main and Wolfert would have given anything for the rummaging of the ponderous sea-chest, which his imagination crammed full of golden chalices, crucifixes, and jolly round bags of doubloons.

The dead stillness that had fallen upon the company was at length interrupted by the stranger, who pulled out a prodigious watch of curious and ancient workmanship, and which in Wolfert's eyes had a decidedly Spanish look. On touching a spring it struck ten o'clock; upon which the sailor called for his reckoning, and having paid it out of a handful of outlandish coin, without taking leave of any one, he rolled out of the room, muttering to himself, as he stamped upstairs to his chamber. It was some time before the company could recover from the silence into which they had been thrown. The very footsteps of the stranger, which were heard now and then as he traversed his chamber, inspired awe.

IN SHINING ARMOR

Still the conversation in which they had been engaged was too interesting not to be resumed. A heavy thunder-gust had gathered up unnoticed, while they were lost in talk, and the torrents of rain that fell forbade all thoughts of setting off for home until the storm should subside. They drew nearer together, therefore, and entreated the worthy Peechy Prauw to continue the tale which had been interrupted. He readily complied, whispering, however, in a tone scarcely above his breath, and drowned occasionally by the rolling of the thunder; and he would pause every now and then, and listen with evident awe, as he heard the heavy footsteps of the stranger pacing overhead.

THE ADVENTURE OF SAM THE BLACK FISHERMAN

Everybody knows Black Sam, the old negro fisherman, or, as he is commonly called, Mud Sam, who has fished about the Sound for the last half century. It is now many years since Sam, having finished his day's work at an early hour, was fishing, one still summer evening, just about the neighborhood of Hell-gate.

He was in a light skiff; and being well acquainted with the currents and eddies, had shifted his station according to the shifting of the tide; but in the eagerness of his sport he did not see that the tide was rapidly ebbing until the roaring of the whirl-pools and eddies warned him of his danger; and he had some difficulty in shooting his skiff from among the rocks and breakers, and getting to the point of Blackwell's Island. Here he cast anchor for some time, waiting the turn of the tide to enable him to return homewards. As the night set in, it grew blustering and gusty. Dark clouds came bundling up in the west; and now and then a growl of thunder or a flash of lightning told that a summer storm was at hand. Sam pulled over, therefore, under the lee of Manhattan Island, and coasting along, came to a snug nook, just under a steep beetling rock, where he fastened his skiff to the root of a tree that shot out from a cleft, and spread its broad branches like a canopy over the water. The gust came scouring along; the wind threw up the river in white surges; the rain rattled among the leaves; the thunder bellowed worse than that which is now bellowing; the lightning seemed to lick up the surges of the stream; but Sam, snugly sheltered under rock and tree, lay crouching in his skiff, rocking upon the billows until he fell asleep. When he woke all was quiet. The gust had passed away, and only now and then a faint gleam of lightning in the east showed which way it had gone. The night was dark and moonless; and from the state of the tide Sam concluded it was near midnight. He was on the point of making loose his skiff to return homewards, when he saw a light gleaming along the water from a distance, which seemed rapidly approaching. As it drew near he perceived it came from a lantern in the bow of a boat gliding along under shadow of the land. It pulled up in a small cove, close to where he was. A man jumped on shore, and searching about with the lantern, exclaimed, "This is the place—here's the iron ring!" The boat was then made fast, and the man returning on board, assisted his comrades in conveying something heavy on shore. As the light gleamed among them, Sam saw that they were five stout desperate-looking fellows, in red woolen caps, with a leader in a three-cornered hat, and that some of them were armed with dirks, or long knives, and pistols. They talked low to one another in some outlandish tongue which he could not understand.

On landing they made their way among the bushes, taking turns to relieve each other in lugging their burden up the rocky bank. Sam's curiosity was now fully aroused; so leaving his skiff he clambered silently up a ridge that overlooked their path. They had stopped to rest for a moment, and the leader was looking about among the bushes with his lantern. "Have you brought the spades?" said one. "They are here," replied another, who had them on his shoulder. "We must dig deep, where there will be no risk of discovery," said a third.

IN SHINING ARMOR

A cold chill ran through Sam's veins. He fancied he saw before him a gang of murderers, about to bury their victim. His knees smote together. In his agitation he shook the branch of a tree with which he was supporting himself as he looked over the edge of the cliff.

"What's that?" cried one of the gang.—"Some one stirs among the bushes!" The lantern was held up in the direction of the noise. One of the red-caps cocked a pistol, and pointed it toward the very place where Sam was standing. He stood motionless—breathless! Fortunately his dingy complexion was in his favor, and made no glare among the leaves.

" 'Tis no one," said the man with the lantern. "What a plague! you would not fire off your pistol and alarm the country!"

The pistol was uncocked; the burden was resumed, and the party slowly toiled along the bank. Sam watched them as they went; the light sending back fitful gleams through the dripping bushes, and it was not till they were fairly out of sight that he ventured to draw breath freely. He now thought of getting back to his boat, and making his escape out of the reach of such dangerous neighbors; but curiosity was all-powerful. He hesitated and lingered and listened. By and by he heard the strokes of spades,—"they are digging a grave!" said he to himself; and the cold sweat started upon his forehead. Every stroke of a spade, as it sounded through the silent groves, went to his heart; it was evident there was as little noise made as possible; everything had an air of terrible mystery and secrecy. Sam could not resist an impulse, in spite of every danger, to steal nearer to the scene of mystery, and overlook the midnight fellows at their work. He crawled along cautiously, therefore, inch by inch; stepping with the utmost care among the dry leaves, lest their rustling should betray him. He came at length to where a steep rock intervened between him and the gang; for he saw the light of their lantern shining up against the branches of the trees on the other side.

Sam slowly and silently clambered up the surface of the rock, and raising his head above its naked edge, beheld the villains immediately below him, and so near, that though he dreaded discovery, he dared not withdraw lest the least movement should be heard. In this way he remained, with his round black face peering above the edge of the rock, like the sun just emerging above the edge of the horizon, or the round-cheeked moon on the dial of a clock.

The red-caps had nearly finished their work; the grave was filled up, and they were carefully replacing the turf. This done, they scattered dry leaves over the place. "And now," said the leader, "I defy the devil himself to find it out."

"The murderers!" exclaimed Sam, involuntarily.

The whole gang started, and looking up, beheld the round black head of Sam just above them. His white eyes strained half out of their orbits; his white teeth chattering, and his whole visage shining with cold perspiration.

"We're discovered!" cried one.

"Down with him!" cried another.

Sam heard the cocking of a pistol, but did not pause for the report. He scrambled over rock and stone, through brush and brier; rolled down banks like a hedgehog; scrambled up others like a catamount. In every direction he heard some one or other of the gang hemming him in. At length he reached the rocky ridge along the river; one of the red-caps was hard behind him. A steep rock like a wall rose directly in his way; it seemed to cut off all retreat, when fortunately he espied the strong cord-like branch of a grape-vine reaching half way down it. He sprang at it with the force of a desperate man, seized it with both hands, and being young and agile, succeeded in swinging himself to the summit of the cliff. Here he stood in full relief against the sky, when the red-cap cocked his pistol and fired. The ball whistled by Sam's head. With the lucky thought of a man in an emergency, he uttered a yell, fell to the ground, and detached at the same time a fragment of the rock, which tumbled with a loud splash into the river.

"I've done his business," said the red-cap to one or two of his comrades as they arrived panting. "He'll tell no tales, except to the fishes in the river."

His pursuers now turned to meet their companions. Sam, sliding silently down the surface of the rock, let himself quietly into his skiff, cast loose the fastening, and abandoned himself to the rapid current, which in that place runs like a mill-stream, and soon swept him off from the neighborhood. It was not, however, until he had drifted a great distance that he ventured to ply his oars, when he made his skiff dart like an arrow through the strait of Hell-gate, nor did he feel himself thoroughly secure until safely nestled in bed in the cockloft of the ancient house of the Suydams.

Here the worthy Peechy Prauw paused to take breath and to take a sip of the gossip tankard that stood at his elbow. His auditors remained with open mouths and outstretched necks, gaping like a nest of swallows for an additional mouthful.

"And did Sam never find out what was buried by the red-caps?" said Wolfert, eagerly, whose mind was haunted by nothing but ingots and doubloons.

"Not that I know of," said Peechy; "but the ghost of the dead man haunts in the neighborhood to this very day. Has none of you

heard of Father Red-cap who haunts the old burnt farmhouse in the woods, on the border of the Sound, near Hell-gate?"

"Oh, to be sure, I've heard tell of something of the kind, but then I took it for some old wives' fable."

"Old wives' fable or not," said Peechy Prauw, "that farm-house stands hard by the very spot. It's been unoccupied time out of mind, and stands in a lonely part of the coast; but those who fish in the neighborhood have often heard strange noises there. Lights have been seen about the wood at night, and an old fellow in a red cap has been seen at the windows more than once, which people take to be the ghost of the body buried there. Once upon a time three soldiers took shelter in the building for the night, and rummaged it from top to bottom, when they found old Father Red-cap astride of a cider-barrel in the cellar, with a jug in one hand and a goblet in the other. He offered them a drink out of his goblet, but just as one of the soldiers was putting it to his mouth—whew! a flash of fire blazed through the cellar, blinded every mother's son of them, and when they recovered their eye-sight, jug, goblet, and Red-cap had vanished, and nothing but the empty cider-barrel remained."

The deep interest taken in this conversation by the company had made them unconscious of the uproar abroad among the elements, when suddenly they were electrified by a tremendous clap of thunder. A lumbering crash followed instantaneously, shaking the building to its very foundation. All started from their seats, imagining it the shock of an earthquake, or that old Father Red-cap was coming among them in all his terrors. They listened for a moment, but only heard the rain pelting against the windows, and the wind howling among the trees.

IN SHINING ARMOR

A sullen pause of the storm, which now rose and sank in gusts, produced a momentary stillness. In this interval the report of a musket was heard, and a long shout, almost like a yell, resounded from the shore. Every one crowded to the window; another musket-shot was heard, and another long shout, mingled wildly with a rising blast of wind. It seemed as if the cry came up from the bosom of the waters; for though incessant flashes of lightning spread a light about the shore, no one was to be seen.

Suddenly the window of the room overhead was opened, and a loud halloo uttered by the mysterious stranger. Several hailings passed from one party to the other, but in a language which none of the company in the bar-room could understand; and presently they heard the window closed, and a great noise overhead, as if all the furniture were pulled and hauled about the room. The negro servant was summoned, and shortly afterwards was seen assisting the veteran to lug the ponderous sea-chest down-stairs.

The landlord was in amazement. "What, you are not going on the water in such a storm?"

"Storm!" said the other, scornfully, "do you call such a sputter of weather a storm?"

"You'll get drenched to the skin," said Peechy affectionately.

"Thunder and lightning!" exclaimed the veteran, "don't preach about weather to a man that has cruised in whirlwinds and tornadoes!"

The obsequious Peechy was again struck dumb. The voice from the water was heard once more in a tone of impatience; the by-standers stared with redoubled awe at this man of storms, who seemed to have come up out of the deep, and to be summoned back to it again. As, with the assistance of the negro, he slowly bore his ponderous sea-chest towards the shore, they eyed it with a superstitious feeling,—half doubting whether he were not really about to embark upon it and launch forth upon the wild waves. They followed him at a distance with a lantern.

"Dowse the light!" roared the hoarse voice from the water, "No one wants light here!"

"Thunder and lightning!" exclaimed the veteran, turning short upon them; "back to the house with you!"

Wolfert and his companions shrunk back in dismay. Still their curiosity would not allow them entirely to withdraw. A long sheet of lightning now flickered across the waves, and discovered a boat, filled with men, just under a rocky point, rising and sinking with the heaving surges, and swashing the waters at every heave. It was with difficulty held to the rocks by a boathook, for the current rushed furiously round the point. The veteran hoisted one end of the lumbering sea-chest on the gunwale of the boat, and seized the handle at the other end to lift it in, when the motion propelled the boat from the shore; the chest slipped off from the gunwale, and, sinking into the waves, pulled the veteran headlong after it. A loud shriek was uttered by all on shore, and a volley of execrations by those on board; but boat and man were hurried away by the rushing swiftness of the tide. A pitchy darkness succeeded; Wolfert Webber indeed fancied that he distinguished a cry for help, and that he beheld the drowning man beckoning for assistance; but when the lightning again gleamed along the water, all was void; neither man nor boat was to be seen; nothing but the dashing and weltering of the waves as they hurried past.

IN SHINING ARMOR

The company returned to the tavern to await the subsiding of the storm. They resumed their seats, and gazed on each other with dismay. The whole transaction had not occupied five minutes, and not a dozen words had been spoken.

"He came," said the landlord, "in a storm, and he went in a storm; he came in the night, and he went in the night; he came nobody knows whence, and he has gone nobody knows where. For aught I know he has gone to sea once more on his chest, and may land to bother some people on the other side of the world."

The thunder-gust which had hitherto detained the company came at length to an end. The cuckoo clock in the hall told midnight; everyone pressed to depart, for seldom was such a late hour of the night trespassed on by these quiet burghers. As they sallied forth, they found the heavens once more serene. The storm which had lately obscured them had rolled away, and lay piled up in fleecy masses on the horizon, lighted up by the bright crescent of the moon, which looked like a little silver lamp hung up in a palace of clouds.

Wolfert Webber had now carried home a fresh stock of stories and notions to ruminate upon. These accounts of pots of money and Spanish treasures, buried here and there and everywhere, about the rocks and bays of these wild shores, made him almost dizzy. As he turned over in his thoughts all that had been told of the singular adventure of the negro fisherman, his imagination gave a totally different complexion to the tale. He saw in the gang of red-caps nothing but a crew of pirates burying their spoils, and his cupidity was once more awakened by the possibility of at length getting on the traces of some of this lurking wealth. Indeed, his infected fancy tinged everything with gold. Caskets of buried jewels, chests of ingots, and barrels of outlandish coins, seemed to court him from their concealments, and supplicate him to relieve them from their untimely graves.

On making private inquiries about the grounds said to be

haunted by Father Red-cap, he was more and more confirmed in his surmise. He learned that the place had several times been visited by experienced money-diggers, who had heard Black Sam's story, though none of them had met with success.

Wolfert Webber was now in a worry of trepidation and impatience, fearful lest some rival adventurer should get a scent of the buried gold. He determined privately to seek out the black fisherman, and get him to serve as guide to the place where he had witnessed the mysterious scene of interment. Sam was easily found. Wolfert found him at his cabin, which was not much larger than a tolerable dog-house. It was rudely constructed of fragments of wrecks and drift-wood, and built on the rocky shore, at the foot of the old fort, just about what at present forms the point of the Battery. A fish-like smell pervaded the place.

Many years had passed away since the time of Sam's youthful adventure, and the snows of many a winter had grizzled the knotty wool upon his head. He perfectly recollected the circumstances, however, for he had often been called upon to relate them. Wolfert's only wish was to secure the old fisherman as a pilot to the spot; and this was readily effected. The long time that had intervened since his nocturnal adventure had effaced all Sam's awe of the place.

The tide was adverse to making the expedition by water, and Wolfert was too impatient to get to the land of promise, to wait for its turning; they set off, therefore, by land. A walk of four or five miles brought them to the edge of a wood, which at that time covered the greater part of the eastern side of the island. Here they struck into a long lane, straggling among trees and bushes, very much overgrown with weeds and mullein-stalks, as if but seldom used, and so completely overshadowed as to enjoy but a kind of twilight. Wild vines entangled the trees and flaunted in their faces; brambles and briers caught their clothes as they passed; the garter-snake glided across their path;

the spotted toad hopped and waddled before them, and the restless catbird mewed at them from every thicket. Had Wolfert Webber been deeply read in romantic legend, he might have fancied himself entering upon forbidden, enchanted ground; or that these were some of the guardians set to keep watch upon buried treasure. As it was, the loneliness of the place, and the wild stories connected with it, had their effect upon his mind.

On reaching the lower end of the lane, they found themselves near the shore of the Sound in a kind of amphitheatre, surrounded by forest-trees. The area had once been a grass-plot, but was now shagged with briers and rank weeds. At one end, and just on the river bank, was a ruined building, little better than a heap of rubbish, with a stack of chimneys rising like a solitary tower out of the centre.

Wolfert had not a doubt that this was the haunted house of Father Red-cap, and called to mind the story of Peechy Prauw. The evening was approaching, and the light falling dubiously among the woody places, gave a melancholy tone to the scene. The nighthawk, wheeling about in the highest regions of the air, emitted his peevish, boding cry. The woodpecker gave a lonely tap now and then on some hollow tree, and the fire-bird streamed by them with his deep-red plumage.

They now came to an enclosure that had once been a garden. It extended along the foot of a rocky ridge, but was little better than a wilderness of weeds, with here and there a matted rose-bush, or a peach or plum tree grown wild and ragged and covered with moss. At the lower end of the garden they passed a kind of vault in the side of a bank, facing the water. It had the look of a root-house. The door, though decayed, was still strong, and appeared to have been recently patched. Wolfert pushed it open. It gave a harsh grating on its hinges, and striking something like a box, a rattling sound ensued, and a skull rolled on the floor. Wolfert drew back shuddering, but was informed by the negro that this was a family vault, belonging to one of the old Dutch families that owned this estate; an assertion corroborated by the sight of coffins of various sizes piled within. Sam had been familiar with all these scenes when a boy, and now knew that he could not be far from the place of which they were in quest.

They now made their way to the water's edge, scrambling along ledges of rocks that overhung the waves, and obliged often to hold by shrubs and grape-vines to avoid slipping into the deep and hurried stream. At length they came to a small cove, or rather indent of the shore. It was protected by steep rocks, and overshadowed by a thick copse of oaks and chestnuts, so as to be sheltered and almost concealed. The negro paused; raised his remnant of a hat, and scratched his grizzled poll for a moment, as he regarded this nook; then suddenly clapping his hands, he stepped exultingly forward, and pointed to a large iron ring, stapled firmly in the rock, just where a broad shelf of stone furnished a commodious landing place. It was the very spot where the red-caps had landed. Years had changed the more perishable features of the scene; but rock and iron yield slowly to the influence of time. On looking more closely, Wolfert remarked three crosses cut in the rock just above the ring, which had no doubt some mysterious signification. Old Sam now readily recognized the overhanging rock under which his skiff had been sheltered during the thunder-gust. To follow up the course which the midnight gang had taken, however, was a harder task. His mind had been so much taken up on that eventful occasion by the persons of the drama, as to pay but little attention to the scenes; and these places look so different by night and day. After wandering about for some time, however, they came to an opening among the trees which Sam thought resembled the place. There was a ledge of rock of moderate height like a wall on one side, which he thought might be the very ridge whence he had overlooked the diggers. Wolfert examined it narrowly, and at length discovered three crosses similar to those on the above ring, cut deeply into the face of the rock, but nearly obliterated by moss that had grown over them. His heart leaped with joy, for he doubted not they were the private marks of the buccaneers. All now that remained was to ascertain the precise spot where the treasure lay buried; for otherwise he might dig at random in the neighborhood of the crosses without coming upon the spoils, and he had already had enough of such profitless labor. Here, however, the old negro was perfectly at a loss, and indeed perplexed him by a variety of opinions; for his recollections were all confused. Sometimes he declared it must have been at the foot of a mulberry tree hard by; then beside a great white stone; then under a small green knoll, a short distance from the ledge; until at length Wolfert became as bewildered as himself.

The shadows of evening were now spreading themselves over the woods, and rock and tree began to mingle together. It was evidently too late to attempt anything farther at present; and, indeed, Wolfert had come unprovided with implements to prosecute his researches. Satisfied, therefore, with having ascertained the place, he took note of all its landmarks, that he might recognize it again, and set out on his return homewards, resolved to prosecute this golden enterprise without delay.

The leading anxiety which had hitherto absorbed every feeling, being now in some measure appeased, fancy began to wander,

and to conjure up a thousand shapes and chimeras as he returned through this haunted region. Pirates hanging in chains seemed to swing from every tree and he almost expected to see some Spanish Don with his throat cut from ear to ear, rising slowly out of the ground and shaking the ghost of a money bag! Their way back lay through the desolate garden, and Wolfert's nerves had arrived at so sensitive a state that the flitting of a bird, the rustling of a leaf, or the falling of a nut, was enough to startle him. As they entered the confines of the garden, they caught sight of a figure at a distance advancing slowly up one of the walks, and bending under the weight of a burden. They paused and regarded him attentively. He wore what appeared to be a woolen cap, and, still more alarming, of a most sanguinary red.

The figure moved slowly on, ascended the bank, and stopped at the very door of the sepulchral vault. Just before entering it he looked around. What was the affright of Wolfert when he recognized the grisly visage of the drowned buccaneer! He uttered an ejaculation of horror. The figure slowly raised his iron fist, and shook it with a terrible menace. Wolfert did not pause to see any more, but hurried off as fast as his legs could carry him, nor was Sam slow in following at his heels. Away, then, did they scramble through bush and brake, nor did they pause to breathe, until they had blundered their way through this perilous wood, and fairly reached the high road to the city.

Several days elapsed before Wolfert could summon courage enough to prosecute the enterprise, so much had he been dismayed by the apparition, whether living or dead, of the grisly buccaneer. In the meantime, what a conflict of mind did he suffer! He neglected all his concerns, wandered in his thoughts and words.

IN SHINING ARMOR

He fancied himself engaged in money-digging; threw the bedclothes right and left, in the idea that he was shovelling away the dirt; groped under the bed in quest of the treasure, and lugged forth, as he supposed, an inestimable pot of gold!

Dame Webber and her daughter were in despair at what they conceived a returning touch of insanity. There are two family oracles, one or other of which Dutch house-wives consult in all cases of great doubt and perplexity—the dominie and the doctor. In the present instance they repaired to the doctor. There was at that time a little dark mouldy man of medicine, famous among the old wives of the Manhattoes for his skill, not only in the healing art, but in all matters of strange and mysterious nature. His name was Dr. Knipperhausen, but he was more commonly known by the appellation of the High-German Doctor. To him did the poor women repair for counsel and assistance.

They found the doctor seated in his little study, clad in his dark camlet robe of knowledge, with his black velvet cap; a pair of green spectacles set in black horn upon his clubbed nose, and poring over a German folio that seemed to reflect back the darkness of his physiognomy. The doctor listened to their statement of the symptoms of Wolfert's malady with profound attention; but when they came to mention his raving about buried money, the little man pricked up his ears. Alas, poor women, they little knew the aid they had called in!

Dr. Knipperhausen had been half his life engaged in seeking the short cuts to fortune, in quest of which so many a long life-time is wasted. His mind therefore had become stored with all kinds of mystic lore; he had dabbled a little in astrology, alchemy, divination; knew how to detect stolen money, and to tell where springs of water lay hidden; in a word, by the dark nature of his knowledge he had acquired the name of the High-German Doctor, which is pretty nearly equivalent to that of necromancer. The doctor had often heard rumors of treasure being buried in various parts of the island, and had long been anxious to get on the traces of it. So far from curing, the doctor caught the malady from his patient. The circumstances unfolded to him awakened all his cupidity; he had not a doubt of money being buried some-where in the neighborhood of the mysterious crosses, and offered to join Wolfert in the search. He informed him that much secrecy and caution must be observed in enterprises of the kind; that money is only to be digged for at night; with certain forms and ceremonies, and burning of drugs; the repeating of mystic words, and, above all, that the seekers must first be provided with a divining rod, which had the wonderful property of pointing to the very spot in the surface of the earth under which treasure lay hidden. As the doctor had given much of his mind to these mat-ters, he charged himself with all the necessary preparations, and, as the quarter of the moon was propitious, he undertook to have the divining rod ready by a certain night. Wolfert's heart leaped with joy at having met with so able a coadjutor. Everything went on secretly, but swimmingly; and the black fisherman was engaged to take them in his skiff to the scene of enterprise.

At length the appointed night arrived for this perilous under-taking. Before Wolfert left his home he counselled his wife and daughter to go to bed, and feel no alarm if he should not return during the night. Like reasonable women, on being told not to feel alarm they fell immediately into a panic. They saw at once by his manner that something unusual was in agitation; all their fears about the unsettled state of his mind were revived with ten-fold force; they hung about him, entreating him not to expose himself to the night air, but all in vain. When once Wolfert was mounted on his hobby, it was no easy matter to get him out of the saddle. It was a clear starlight night, when he issued out of the portal of the Webber palace. He wore a large flapped hat tied under the chin with a handkerchief of his daughter's, to secure him from the night damp, while Dame Webber threw her long red cloak about his shoulders, and fastened it round his neck.

The doctor had been no less carefully armed and accoutred, and sallied forth in his camlet robe, a thick clasped book under his arm, a basket of drugs and dried herbs in one hand, and in the other the miraculous rod of divination.

The great church-clock struck ten as Wolfert and the doctor passed by the church-yard, and the watchman bawled in hoarse voice a long and doleful "All's well!" A deep sleep had already fallen upon this primitive little burgh, nothing disturbed this awful silence, excepting now and then the bark of some profligate night-walking dog, or the serenade of some romantic cat. It is true, Wolfert fancied more than once that he heard the sound of a stealthy footfall at a distance behind them; but it might have been merely the echo of their own steps along the quiet streets. He thought also at one time that he saw a tall figure skulking after them—stopping when they stopped, and moving on as they proceeded; but the dim and uncertain lamp-light threw such vague gleams and shadows, that this might all have been mere fancy.

They found the old fisherman waiting for them, smoking his pipe in the stern of the skiff, which was moored just in front of his little cabin. A pickaxe and spade were lying in the bottom of the boat, with a dark lantern and a jug of good Dutch courage.

Thus then did these three worthies embark in their cockle-shell of a skiff upon this nocturnal expedition, with a wisdom and valor equalled only by the three wise men of Gotham, who adventured to sea in a bowl. The tide was rising and running rapidly up the Sound. The current bore them along, almost without the aid of an oar. The profile of the town lay all in shadow. Here and there a light feebly glimmered from some sick-chamber, or from the cabin-window of some vessel at anchor in the stream. Not a cloud obscured the deep starry firmament, the lights of which wavered on the surface of the placid river; and a shooting meteor, streaking its pale course in the very direction they were taking, was interpreted by the doctor into a most propitious omen.

In a little while they glided by the point of Corlaer's Hook with the rural inn which had been the scene of such night adventures. Wolfert felt a chill pass over him as they passed the point where the buccaneer had disappeared. He pointed it out to Dr. Knipperhausen. While regarding it, they thought they saw a boat actually lurking at the very place; but the shore cast such a shadow over the border of the water that they could discern nothing distinctly. They had not proceeded far when they heard the low sounds of distant oars, as if cautiously pulled. Sam plied his oars with redoubled vigor, and knowing all the eddies and currents of the stream, soon left their followers, if such they were, far astern. In a little while they stretched across Turtle Bay and Kip's Bay, then shrouded themselves in the deep shadows of the Manhattan shore, and glided swiftly along, secure from observation. At length the negro shot his skiff into a little cove, darkly embowered by trees, and made it fast to the well-known iron ring. They now landed, and lighting the lantern, gathered their various implements and proceeded slowly through the bushes. Every sound startled them, even that of their own footsteps among the dry leaves; and the hooting of a screech owl, from the shattered chimney of the neighboring ruin, made their blood run cold.

In spite of all Wolfert's caution in taking note of the landmarks, it was some time before they could find the open place among the trees, where the treasure was supposed to be buried. At length they came to the ledge of rock; and on examining its surface by the aid of the lantern, Wolfert recognized the three mystic crosses. Their hearts beat quick, for the momentous trial was at hand that was to determine their hopes.

The lantern was now held by Wolfert Webber, while the doctor produced the divining rod. It was a forked twig, one end of which was grasped firmly in each hand, while the centre, forming the stem, pointed perpendicularly upwards. The doctor moved his wand about, within a certain distance of the earth, from place to place, but for some time without any effect, while Wolfert kept the light of the lantern turned full upon it, and watched it with the most breathless interest. At length the rod began slowly to turn. The doctor grasped it with greater earnestness, his hands trembling with the agitation of his mind. The wand continued to turn gradually, until at length the stem had reversed its position, and pointed perpendicularly downward, and remained pointing to one spot as fixedly as the needle to the pole.

"This is the spot!" said the doctor, in an almost inaudible tone.

Wolfert's heart was in his throat.

"Shall I dig?" said the negro, grasping the spade.

"*Pots tausend, no!*" replied the little doctor, hastily. He now ordered his companions to keep close by him, and to maintain the most inflexible silence. That certain precautions must be taken and ceremonies used to prevent the evil spirits which kept about buried treasure from doing them any harm. He then drew a circle about the place, enough to include the whole party. He next gathered dry twigs and leaves and made a fire, upon which he threw certain drugs and dried herbs which he had brought in his basket. A thick smoke arose, diffusing a potent odor, savoring marvellously of brimstone and assafoetida, which, however grateful it might be to the olfactory nerves of spirits, nearly strangled poor Wolfert, and produced a fit of coughing and wheezing that made the whole grove resound. Dr. Knipperhausen then unclasped the volume which he had brought under his arm, which was printed in red and black characters in German text. While Wolfert held the lantern, the doctor, by the aid of his spectacles, read off several forms of conjuration in Latin and German. He then ordered Sam to seize the pickaxe and proceed to work. The close-bound soil gave obstinate signs of not having been disturbed for many a year. After having picked his way through the surface, Sam came to a bed of sand and gravel, which he threw briskly to right and left with the spade.

"Hark!" said Wolfert, who fancied he heard a trampling among the dry leaves, and a rustling through the bushes. Sam paused for a moment, and they listened. No footstep was near. The bat flitted by them in silence; a bird, roused from its roost by the light which glared up among the trees, flew circling about the flame. In the profound stillness of the woodland, they could distinguish the current rippling along the rocky shore, and the distant murmuring and roaring of Hell-gate.

The negro continued his labors, and had already digged a considerable hole. The doctor stood on the edge, reading formulae every now and then from his black-letter volume, or throwing more drugs and herbs upon the fire; while Wolfert bent anxiously over the pit, watching every stroke of the spade. Any one witnessing the scene thus lighted up by fire, lantern, and the reflection of Wolfert's red mantle might have mistaken the little doctor for some magician busied in his incantations, and the grizzly-headed negro for some swart goblin, obedient to his commands.

IN SHINING ARMOR

At length the spade of the fisherman struck upon something that sounded hollow. The sound vibrated to Wolfert's heart. He struck his spade again.

" 'Tis a chest," said Sam.

"Full of gold, I'll warrant it!" cried Wolfert, clasping his hands with rapture.

Scarcely had he uttered the words when a sound from above caught his ear. He cast up his eyes, and lo! by the expiring light of the fire he beheld, just above the disk of the rock, what appeared to be the grim visage of the drowned buccaneer, grinning hideously down upon him.

Wolfert gave a loud cry, and let fall the lantern. His panic communicated itself to his companions. The negro leaped out of the hole; the doctor dropped his book and basket, and began to pray in German. All was horror and confusion. The fire was scattered about, the lantern extinguished. In their hurry-scurry they ran against and confounded one another. They fancied a legion of hobgoblins let loose upon them, and that they saw, by the fitful gleams of the scattered embers, strange figures, in red caps, gibbering and ramping around them. The doctor ran one way, the negro another, and Wolfert made for the water side. As he plunged struggling onwards through brush and brake, he heard the tread of some one in pursuit. He scrambled frantically forward. The footsteps gained upon him. He felt himself grasped by his cloak, when suddenly his pursuer was attacked in turn. A fierce fight and struggle ensued—a pistol was discharged that lit up rock and bush for a second, and showed two figures grappling together—all was then darker than ever. The contest continued—the combatants clinched each other, and panted, and groaned, and rolled among the rocks. There was snarling and growling as of a cur, mingled with curses, in which Wolfert fancied he could recognize the voice of the buccaneer. He would fain have fled, but he was on the brink of a precipice, and could go no further.

Again the parties were on their feet; again there was a tugging and struggling, as if strength alone could decide the combat, until one was precipitated from the brow of the cliff, and sent headlong into the deep stream that whirled below. Wolfert heard the plunge, and a kind of bubbling murmur, but the darkness of the night hid everything from him, and the swiftness of the current swept everything instantly out of hearing. One of the combatants was disposed of, but whether friend or foe, Wolfert could not tell, nor whether they might not both be foes. He heard the survivor approach, and his terror revived. He saw, where the profile of the rocks rose against the horizon, a human form advancing. He could not be mistaken! it must be the buccaneer. Whither should he fly!—a precipice was on one side—a murderer on the other. The enemy approached—he was close at hand. Wolfert attempted to let himself down the face of the cliff. His cloak caught in a thorn that grew on the edge. He was jerked from off his feet, and held dangling in the air, half choked by the string with which his careful wife had fastened the garment around his neck. Wolfert thought his last moment had arrived; when the string broke, and he tumbled down the bank, bumping from rock to rock, and bush to bush, and leaving the red cloak fluttering like a banner in the air.

It was a long while before Wolfert came to himself. When he opened his eyes, the ruddy streaks of morning were already shooting up the sky. He found himself grievously battered, and lying in the bottom of a boat. He attempted to sit up, but was too sore and stiff to move. A voice requested him in friendly accents to lie still. He turned his eyes towards the speaker; it was Dirk Waldron. He had dogged the party, at the earnest request of Dame Webber and her daughter. Dirk had been completely distanced in following the light skiff of the fisherman, and had just come in to rescue the poor money-digger from his pursuer.

Thus ended this perilous enterprise. The doctor and Black Sam severally found their way back to the Manhattoes, each having some dreadful tale of peril to relate. As to poor Wolfert, instead of returning in triumph laden with bags of gold, he was borne home on a shutter, followed by a rabble-rout of curious urchins. His wife and daughter saw the dismal pageant from a distance, and alarmed the neighborhood with their cries. The whole town was in a buzz with the story of the money-diggers. Many repaired to the scene of the previous night's adventures; but though they found the very place of the digging, they discovered nothing that compensated them for their trouble. Some say they found the fragments of an oaken chest, and an iron pot-lid, which savored strongly of hidden money; and that in the old family vault there were traces of bales and boxes; but this is all very dubious.

In fact, the secret of all this story has never to this day been discovered; whether any treasure were ever actually buried at that place; whether, if so, it were carried off at night by those who had buried it; or whether it still remains there under the guardianship of gnomes and spirits until it shall be properly sought for, is all matter of conjecture.

There were many conjectures formed, also, as to who and what was the strange man of the seas who had domineered over the little fraternity at Corlaer's Hook for a time; disappeared so strangely, and reappeared so fearfully. Some supposed him a smuggler sta-tioned at that place to assist his comrades in landing their goods among the rocky coves of the island. Others, that he was one of the ancient comrades of Kidd or Bradish, returned to convey away treasures formerly hidden in the vicinity. The only circumstance that throws anything like a vague light on this mysterious matter, is a report which prevailed of a strange foreign-built shallop, with much the look of a picaroon, having been seen hovering about the Sound for several days without landing or reporting herself, though boats were seen going to and from her at night; and that she was seen standing out of the mouth of the harbor, in the gray of the dawn, after the catastrophe of the money-diggers. I must not omit to mention another report, also, of the buccaneer, who was supposed to have been drowned, being seen before daybreak with a lantern in his hand, seated astride of his great sea-chest, and sailing through Hell-gate, which just then began to roar and bellow with redoubled fury.

While all the gossip world was thus filled with talk and rumor, poor Wolfert lay sick and sorrowful in his bed, bruised in body and sorely beaten down in mind. His wife and daughter did all they could to bind up his wounds, both corporal and spiritual. The good old dame never stirred from his bedside, where she sat knitting from morning till night; while his daughter busied herself about him with the fondest care. It was a moving sight to behold him wasting away day by day; growing thinner and thinner, and staring with rueful visage from under an old patchwork counterpane.

Dirk Waldron was the only being that seemed to shed a ray of sunshine into this house of mourning. He came in with cheery look and manly spirit, and tried to reanimate the expiring heart of the poor money-digger, but it was all in vain. Wolfert was completely done over. If anything was wanting to complete his despair, it was a notice served upon him in the midst of his distress, that the corporation was about to run a new street through the very centre of his cabbage-garden. He now saw nothing before him but poverty and ruin. His last reliance, the garden of his forefathers, was to be laid waste, and what then was to become of his poor wife and child?

His eyes filled with tears as they followed the dutiful Amy out of the room one morning. Dirk Waldron was seated beside him; Wolfert grasped his hand, pointed after his daughter, and for the first time since his illness, broke the silence he had maintained.

"I am going!" said he, shaking his head feebly, "and when I am gone—my poor daughter—."

"Leave her to me, father!" said Dirk, manfully—"I'll take care of her!"

Wolfert looked up in the face of the cheery, strapping youngster, and saw there was none better able to take care of a woman.

"Enough," said he, "she is yours!—and now fetch me a lawyer and let me make my will and die."

The lawyer was brought—a dapper, bustling, round-headed little man, Roorback (or Rollebuck as it was pronounced) by name. At the sight of him the women broke into loud lamentations. Wolfert made a feeble motion for them to be silent. Poor Amy buried her face and her grief in the bed-curtain. Dame Webber resumed her knitting to hide her distress, which betrayed itself however in a pellucid tear, which trickled silently down, and hung at the end of her peaked nose; while the cat, the only unconcerned member of the family, played with the good dame's ball of worsted, as it rolled about the floor.

Wolfert lay on his back, his night-cap drawn over his forehead; his eyes closed; his whole visage the picture of death. He begged the lawyer to be brief, for he felt his end approaching, and that he had no time to lose. The lawyer nibbed his pen, spread out his paper, and prepared to write.

"I give and bequeath," said Wolfert, faintly, "my small farm"—

"What—all!" exclaimed the lawyer.

Wolfert half opened his eyes and looked upon the lawyer.

"Yes—all," said he.

"What! all the great patch of land with cabbages and sunflowers, which the corporation is just going to run a main street through?"

"The same," said Wolfert, with a heavy sigh, and sinking back upon his pillow.

"I wish him joy that inherits it!" said the little lawyer, chuckling, and rubbing his hands involuntarily.

"What do you mean?" said Wolfert, again opening his eyes.

"That he'll be one of the richest men in the place!" cried little Rollebuck.

The expiring Wolfert seemed to step back from the threshold of existence; his eyes again lighted up; he raised himself in his bed, shoved back his red worsted night-cap, and stared broadly at the lawyer.

"You don't say so!" exclaimed he.

"Faith, but I do!" rejoined the other.—"Why, when that great field and that huge meadow come to be laid out in streets, and cut up into snug building lots—why, whoever owns it need not pull off his hat to the patroon!"

"Say you so?" cried Wolfert, half thrusting one leg out of bed, "why, then I think I'll not make my will yet!"

To the surprise of everybody the dying man actually recovered. The vital spark, which had glimmered faintly in the socket, received fresh fuel from the oil of gladness, which the little lawyer poured into his soul. It once more burnt up into a flame.

Give physic to the heart, ye who would revive the body of a spirit-broken man! In a few days Wolfert left his room; in a few days more his table was covered with deeds, plans of streets, and building-lots. Little Rollebuck was constantly with him, his right hand man and adviser and instead of making his will, assisted in the more agreeable task of making his fortune. In fact Wolfert Webber was one of those worthy Dutch burghers of the Manhattoes whose fortunes have been made, in a manner, in spite of themselves; who have tenaciously held on to their hereditary acres, raising turnips and cabbages about the skirts of the city, hardly able to make both ends meet, until the corporation has cruelly driven streets through their abodes, and they have suddenly awakened out of their lethargy, and, to their astonishment, found themselves rich men.

Before many months had elapsed, a great bustling street

passed through the very center of the Webber garden, just where Wolfert had dreamed of finding a treasure. His golden dream was accomplished; he did indeed find an unlooked-for source of wealth; for, when his paternal lands were distributed into building lots, and rented out to safe tenants, instead of producing a paltry crop of cabbages, they returned him an abundant crop of rent; insomuch that on quarter-day it was a goodly sight to see his tenants knocking at the door, from morning till night, each with a little round-bellied bag of money, a golden produce of the soil.

The ancient mansion of his forefathers was still kept up; but instead of being a little yellow-fronted Dutch house in a garden, it now stood boldly in the midst of a street, the grand home of the neighborhood; for Wolfert enlarged it with a wing on each side, and cupola or tea-room on top, where he might climb up and smoke.

As Wolfert waxed old, and rich, and corpulent, he also set up a great gingerbread-colored carriage, drawn by a pair of black Flanders mares with tails that swept the ground; and to commemorate the origin of his greatness, he had for his crest a full-blown cabbage painted on the panels, with the pithy motto ALLES KOPF, that is to say, ALL HEAD; meaning thereby that he had risen by sheer headwork.

To fill the measure of his greatness, in the fullness of time the renowned Ramm Rapelye slept with his fathers and Wolfert Webber succeeded to the leather-bottomed arm-chair, in the inn-parlor at Corlaer's Hook; where he long reigned greatly honored and respected, insomuch that he was never known to tell a story without its being believed, nor to utter a joke without its being laughed at.

—(Abridged)

151

A Dream of the Middle Ages

From the Italian of The Divine Comedy by Dante Alighieri

In the grim gray streets of Florence, by Arno's shop-lined bridges, May-day brought with merriment the festival of the Spring. The mildness of the sun again reclothed the earth and made her laugh for joy, with manifold little flowerets blooming mid fresh green leaves. Sunlight in narrow streets, glinting athwart the shadows; color running riot against the solemn gray of frowning palace-walls!

In the year of our Lord's birth, 1274, Dante A'li-ghie'ri was ending his ninth year. Going to honor the May at the house of a nobly-born friend, he chanced for the first time to meet a little maid of nine. Beatrice Por-ti-na'ri, her very name meant Blessed! How many people called her so, yet never knew how fitly! A little red dress she wore, made in such a fashion as became her tender years; her eyes were deep and liquid like the deep changing green of the sea; and so young, so sweet she was, she seemed a little angel. In the heart of the boy, secret chambers began to stir with life.

"Love so strong I feel, it is stronger than I," he said. "Behold this love shall rule me!" And from this time forward, love lorded it over his soul and commanded him many times that he should seek to see this beautiful youthful angel, so that he, in his boyhood, often went seeking her, and saw her always of noble, gentle, sweet, and praiseworthy deportment. When he studied with other youths at the feet of learned masters, that one bright dreamlike figure, the figure of Beatrice, wove itself back and forth, across the sober colors of his daily life and thoughts.

Grave and thoughtful of face, as he grew from youth into manhood, he walked in his long flowing robe with quiet step and solemn through the streets of Florence and saw with adoring eye Beatrice, his beloved, coming there to meet him. "This is not a woman, but one of Heaven's angels!" so cried the people who saw her; yet garmented in humility, she showed no vainglory or pride of the praise her beauty awoke. With all the fiery intensity of his fiery Italian soul, Dante loved Beatrice. And then came somber shadows quenching the light of his life. Beatrice was given in marriage to another and in a short time died, so beautiful, so sweet, so young, and so beloved.

Dante tried to forget, to fill his mind and heart. He married another maid and plunged with all his soul into affairs of state. But the great republic of Florence was split by party strife. Poor folk hated the rich and followers of the Emperor brawled in tavern and street with followers of the Pope. Now was a man so proud that his horse went shod with silver; now was the proud brought low, dragged at his horse's heels and murdered at the gate of a convent, or exposed like a beast in a cage, to be jeered at in the market place and to die there of rage and shame. An age of violence it was, an age of untamed passions, and none there was to hearken

153

to the preaching of Fra Gio-van'ni concerning the Kiss of Peace.

Why was the world such a world? Dante in constant surprise challenged the world with that question, while the memory of Beatrice shone brighter still in his heart. Symbol of all things lovely, gentle, sweet, and good,—why could not the world follow such a star? Why did it lie so earthbound hugging its vice and sin?

"It was given me to behold a wonderful vision," he wrote, as he sat and dreamed of Beatrice. "It is my hope that I shall yet write of her what hath not before been written of any woman."

Part of a poem he wrote and laid away in a chest. And then fell a second blow. In his seven and thirtieth year, his foes came into power, and being on a journey to Rome, he heard that he had been banished. His home had been ransacked, his property had been seized, his family left destitute, and he himself doomed to be burned, if ever he set foot again within the gates of Florence.

Florence had cast him out. Henceforth he was homeless, a wanderer on the earth. Fiercely he resented the injustice heaped upon him! When he came to a city's gates he could not but be reminded that into the gates of Florence he could go no more. When he beheld the towers of powerful feudal castles cresting the distant hills, he felt how arrogant are the strong, and how abused the weak. Every brook and river reminded him of the Arno.

"I grieve for all who suffer," he said; "yet have the greater pity for those who being in exile, see their native land only in dreams!"

From patron to patron he wandered, ever onward from place to place. Poor, proud, earnest, moody, he was not one to win the shallow hearts of men. As he tramped the roads of Italy, sorrow-stricken and lonely, his soul, once so soft and tender, froze into proud isolation, and looked out stern and solemn as though imprisoned in ice. His face became the face of one forever in protest, in unsurrendering battle against the evils of the world. Why was the world such a world? Why was it of such a sort? With deep and fiery emphasis, the question still persisted, and in his troubled soul rose great and awful thoughts.

The earthly world had cast him forth; no living heart now loved him. More and more he longed, intensely longed for Beatrice. Before his eyes this time-world fluttered as an unreal shadow; but ever more real to him became that world of the Spirit, where in ineffable glory Beatrice now dwelt. Florence he would never see; but Hell, Purgatory, Heaven, these he would surely see! Thereof, for ten long centuries, the Christian world had dreamed. Good was excellent, high, glorious as light and Heaven. Evil was hideous, dark, black as the depths of Hell. What course of life was good, deserving eternal joy? What course of life was evil, black as the depths of Hell? Homeless on earth, the great soul of Dante made its home more and more in those fiery realms of fancy, placed by the Middle Ages beyond the Gates of Death.

Filled with this, brooding over it in speechless thought and awe, Dante burst forth at length into mystic unfathomable song. He would complete the manuscript he had begun in Florence, which had, as by a miracle, escaped the fury of his foes. Through him the Middle Ages should speak its dreams and visions, speak in rapt sincerity, earnestness and passion.

> Ah! from what agonies of heart and brain,
>   What exultations trampling on despair,
>   What tenderness, what tears, what hate of wrong,
> What passionate outcry of a soul in pain,
>   Uprose this poem of the earth and air,
>   This mediaeval miracle of song!

II

Dante's Voyage to the Inferno, Purgatory and Paradise

Midway upon the journey of my life, I found myself within a forest dark, the path before me lost and all around a wood, so savage, rough, and stern, that but the very thought of it renews my fear. How I had come to such a place I cannot say, so full was I of sleep at that same moment when I turned aside from my true path. But all night long I wandered there within a valley dark and shadowy as death. So came I to a point where suddenly the valley ended and a mountain, difficult and high, barred all my further way. Dark was my heart with shadows as a mountain-tarn at night. Then up I looked and saw the topmost cliffs already touched with sunlight and the morning glow. So was my fear a little quieted and down I sat to rest. But when I had resumed my way, a panther light and swift, with spotted skin, appeared and walked before, and never moved she from before my face.

The time was the beginning of the morning and the sun was mounting up with all those morning stars that were with Him, what time the Love Divine at first in motion set those beauteous things. But on a sudden there appeared a lion terrible. He seemed as if against me he were coming, with head uplifted and with ravenous hunger, so the fiery air seemed full of fear, and after him a she-wolf, lean with famishings. She brought upon me so much fright, that I relinquished hope of climbing up that height and turned in haste to flee. But there before me in the desert-waste a man appeared.

"Have pity on me," unto him I cried; "whichever thou mayst be, a man or shade!"

And he replied to me: "I am not now a man though once I was. I am that poet who did sing of great Ae-ne'as and the fall of Troy. But tell me why thou dost not climb this Mt. Delectable, which is the source and cause of every joy?"

Then much I marveled at who stood before me there and that he called this mount Delectable which unto me so hard and difficult had seemed. With bashful forehead I replied:

"Now art thou Vergil, of all poets honored most by me! Behold the beast from which I flee and save me from her, famous Sage!"

"Yea, I will lead thee by another road," responded he; "I'll lead thee by the way of Hell up Purgatory, and if thou wouldst still further go, a soul more worthy far than I, shall show the way!"

And I to him:—"O master mine, I know that thou dost show me Hell and Purgatory, that I may learn to find escape from all their woes and straightway aim to reach the joys of Paradise."

Then he moved on and there behind I followed in the way. But as I went, I doubted whether I indeed was worthy thus to visit realms where never mortal man had gone. I pressed my doubts upon my guide; he answered thus:—

"Thy soul attainted is with cowardice! Why dost thou think I came to thee? I'll tell thee why. As I resided there in Limbo, a fair and saintly lady called to me. Her eyes were shining brighter than the stars and she began to say with voice angelical: 'O courteous bard, a friend of mine, though not a friend of Fortune, is so beset there on the desert-slope that he has turned through terror and may, I fear, be lost. Bestir thee now and go to aid him. I who bid thee, I am Beatrice. From Paradise I came and there would fain return. Love moved me which compelleth me to speak.' Weeping, her shining eyes she turned away; whereby she made me swifter come. What is it then? Why, why dost thou delay?"

As flowerets by the chill of night bowed down, when first the white sun touches them again, lift up their heads all open on their stems, such I became when thus I heard 'twas Beatrice had sent my guide to me. Now like one unto whom no fear is known, I bade him lead the way, then entered after on the deep and savage path.

> "Through me the way is to the dolorous city,
> Dolorous, dolorous city, city of dole and woe!
> All hope abandon ye who enter here!"

These words in somber color I beheld upon the summit of a gate, and he, my guide, exclaimed: "Behold the place whereof I told thee. Herein dwell those who knew the right but did it not, and have

no sorrow for their sin, but hug it still." He laid his hand on mine to comfort me and led me on among the secret things.

Within the gate, what sighs I heard, complaints, and ululations loud, resounding through the air without a star, whence I, at the beginning wept. Accents of anger, words of agony and voices high and hoarse, with sound of hands, made up a tumult that goes whirling on forever in that air forever black, as whirls the sand when wild the whirlwind breathes. I cried with horror: "Master, pray, what folk is this which seems by pain so vanquished on the very verge of Hell?"

And he to me replied: "These miserable folk are they who had nor courage to do right, nor wrong, those lukewarm folk nor hot nor cold, nor faithful unto God nor to the Devil. Them neither Heaven nor Hell will have—and no worse fate befalleth any man!"

And I beheld a banner whirling restlessly, all shifting and un-stable, and after it so long a train of people that I scarce believed mine eyes. These cowardly wretches, hateful both to God and to his enemies, blind life was theirs! They took no stand for right nor wrong on anything! Now naked, all, they went by gadflies and by hornets stung, yet even so their souls were never pricked to life.

We looked and passed and saw beyond, a crowd of people on a

river's bank, and lo, there coming toward us in a boat an old man hoary with the hair of age, crying: "Woe unto you, ye souls depraved! I come to lead you to the other shore, to the eternal shades in heat and frost!" And he to me cried out: "Thou living soul, go back! I warn thee cross not here unto such woes as these!"

But unto him my Guide explained, "Now vex thee not. 'Tis of the Will Divine he crosses here!" Thereat was quieted that grizzled ferryman with eyes of flame. But all those weary naked souls, from these words hearing of the woe to come, their color changed; they quaked their teeth together cursing God and men. All weeping bitterly, they clung to that accursed shore as to their one last hope. But he, the demon Charon with his burning eyes, did beckon unto them. Collecting them together, with his oar he beat the laggards till they lost their hold and fell. As dead leaves fall in autumn, fluttering, one by one, till all the branch is bare, so scattering, one by one, light, feeble, fluttering, the souls fell from that bank.

This finished, all the field of dusk shuddered, and that so violently, that, of that terror, recollection bathes me still in sweat.

DONN P. CRANE

The land of tears gave forth a blast of wind. With loud tonation flashed a fiery light, which overmastered me in every sense, and as a man whom sleep doth seize, I fell. So was I carried over Ach'er-on while I slept, and when I woke, I found myself upon the brink of Hell whence issued all that thunder of wild sounds. Before me yawned a conical abyss which by nine narrowing terraces did pierce unto the center of the earth. So deep it lay and filled with vapor, that by fixing on its depth my sight, nothing whatever I discerned therein.

"Let us descend now into that blind world;" the poet said.

Within the foremost circle of that deep abyss we heard no cries of torment, only gentle sighs. "Here dwell those well-intentioned ones who lived on earth before Christianity had brought to men its fullest tidings of great joy," my master said. "With these dwell I myself."

Then through a forest of thick-crowding ghosts we went, until I saw a fire that overcame a hemisphere of darkness round about and in that light a noble castle rose. We entered through the gates and so came out upon a meadow which with sharp metallic sheen like green enamel shone, and on that bright enamel people stood and walked about with solemn eyes and slow, of great authority in their countenances. There saw I those whom only to have seen, exalted me,—Hector, Aeneas, Cicero, and all their honored host.

From out the light and quiet of that castle, we now passed again unto the air that shuddered and the place where nothing shines. Down we climbed and down till there before us loomed with lashing tail that dread judge, Minos, who there standeth horribly and snarls. He judgeth all and from his presence they are hurled into those dark and hideous depths that yawn with fire and vapor far below.

And now began the dolesome notes to

grow quite audible unto me. I came unto a place mute of all
light, which bellows as the sea doth in a tempest, if by angry
winds 'tis stirred. That wild infernal hurricane there never rests,
but hurtles spirits onward, whirling ever round and round. Un-
stable they in love, unfaithful in affections, now driven here and
there, as by desires that ever change! No hope have they of rest.
No moment's sweet repose! As cranes go chanting forth their
lays, making in air a long line of themselves, so came they, uttering
lamentations sad. And even as I pitied them, I thus addressed my
guide: "O poet, I would speak unto those two, who, clinging there
together, drift so light upon the wind."

And he to me: "When they draw near, implore them by the love
which leadeth them, and they will come and speak!"

Soon as the wind in our direction swayed them, my voice I did
uplift, and even as turtle-doves, called onward by desire, fly to their

nest with steady wings, so came they, when by love, implored.

Then spake a little flute-like voice with infinite wail that wrung my heart: "O living creature, gracious and benign, since thou hast pity on our woe, we come to speak with thee, while silent is the wind as now. I am Francesca whom thou knewest as a child, she whom her father gave as wife unto the elder lord of Ri'mi-ni, to buy his friendship when great wars were o'er. But he came not to fetch me, he, that elder lord. He sent Pa'o-lo in his stead, his brother young and handsome. Him he sent, Paolo, in his stead! Then love that doth on gentle hearts full swiftly seize, did seize Paolo for the beauty that was mine, and love that doth exempt no maid beloved from loving, seized me with such pleasure of this man, that as thou seest, I do love him still. We saw each other often, for we dwelt beneath one roof, within my husband's house. We loved each other dearly, as young things do ever love. Then came that elder lord, my husband, and finding us together, with his dagger slew us both. Yet even here, amid such woes, we do rejoice that we shall never part!"

These words were borne along from them to us as there they hung together, poised upon the wind. With pity overcome I wept. "How did you two first know you loved?" I cried.

Again that flute-like wail, and she to me: "There is no greater sorrow than to recall in misery the happy time! One day we read of Lancelot, how love for Guinevere did him enthrall when he was sent to bring her to her bridals with King Arthur. Alone we were and without any fear. Full many a time our eyes together drew and drove the color from our faces. But as we read of their first kiss, this man, who ne'er from me shall be divided, kissed me likewise on the mouth. That day no further did we read, . . . "

And all the while Francesca uttered this, that other one, Paolo, wept so sadly, that, for pity, I did swoon away, nor knew when rose the wind again to whirl them off together wailing on its wings.

At the return of consciousness that closed before the pity of those two, I followed further with my guide to deeper terraces of

The fantasia, *Francesca Da Rimini*, by the Russian composer, Tchaïkouvsky, is based on the story of Francesca and Paola, as given in this poem by Dante.

woe and sin; and greater was the woe with every circle down. There saw we gluttons, misers, prodigals, all those who through intemperance of any sort have lacked control. They dwelt in lands of murk and mire and rain eternal, in lands of fog, and stench, and hideous marsh. The violent we saw who did much wrong by force, highwaymen, robbers, conquerors of the world, all sitting in a stream of boiling blood or wandering o'er hot sands in restless herds, while over them, athwart the dark, with gradual steady fall that gave no hope of cease, were raining down dilated flakes of fire, as falls the snow on Alp when winds are still. Without repose forever was the dance of miserable hands and feet, now here, now there, to shake them clear of those live sparks. So danced the violent in Hell.

Thus down and down we went, with steep descent and awful, I afraid at times but by my guide led on and comforted; and all the way was darkness, lit by fire, with monsters here and hornéd demons wielding whips. So came we to the deepest depths of that abyss, the foul and black abode of brutish crime, where lurks such infamy that pity turns to loathing there. There Judas is who did betray the Christ, and traitors all, and Satan, Emperor of that Realm. Here are no flames but only ice. Ice-cold the depths of Hell, ice-cold as hate, indifference, lovelessness, that more than any sin of heat, can kill the soul. And at the very bottom of that pit, like

Symphony after Dante's Divina Commedia by Franz Liszt (1811-1886), mirrors in music, profoundly suited to the poet's theme, Dante's Hell, his Purgatory, and the heavenly bliss of Paradise.

some colossal statue, Satan stands encased in ice, thence issuing only from his mid-breast forth. Three heads he has, and six bat-wings. Sails of the sea I never saw so large. He waved them and three winds proceeded cold therefrom.

No lower could we go than Satan's depths of ice. My guide now bade me cling to him and, laying hold of Satan's side adown his rugged limbs he climbed, then plunged into the opening of a rock, that we might issue forth from Hell. Naught could we see. The cave was dark but water there we heard and let its rippling lead us forth. Then as we mounted, through a small round aperture, dawned on our sight the stars.

Delights did recommence soon as I issued forth from that dead air which had with sadness filled my heart. The lovely planet Venus made the East to laugh and in the flamelets of the Southern Cross, the heavens rejoiced. We stood upon an island whence arose in twilit dusk of morning-stars, a mount as high as Hell is deep, the mount of Purgatory, whereon, climbing up, the human spirit purges, cleans itself, and by repentance for its sins, now to ascend to heaven becometh worthy. Soon, as we stood, came first faint white of Dawn to rout the dusk, and in those pure pale gleams of morning light, now from afar I recognized the trembling of the sea.

IN SHINING ARMOR

We took our way unto the shore. Already had the white and rosy cheeks of lovely Dawn by too great age to yellow turned, when lo, there in the West upon the ocean floor appeared to me a light, along the sea so swiftly coming, that its motion by no flight of wings is equalled. Then my master cried: "Make haste! Make haste to bow the knee! Behold, the Angel of God! Nor oar he wants, nor other sail than his own wings to fly between so distant shores!"

As he came near, the Bird Divine, so radiant did he seem, mine eyes could scarce endure the sight. He came to shore and with him, swift and light, a little vessel, buoyed so lightly up, the water swallowed naught thereof. Upon the stern the Heavenly Pilot stood; beatitude seemed written on his face, and full an hundred spirits sat within the boat, chanting an holy psalm as with one voice.

He made the sign of Holy Rood upon them, whereat all cast

themselves upon the shore, and he departed swiftly as he came.

On every side was darting forth the day; the sun with his resplendent shafts had now from the mid-heavens chased all lingerings of the dark, when with these people in a mighty throng, we started for the mountain's base. Soon had we scattered o'er the way, as each was able there to climb. At times my footsteps lagged, so difficult the path; and I perchance had given up my goal long ere I reached the gate of Purgatory, had my guide not said: "O human creatures, born to soar aloft, why fall ye thus before a little wind? Her shalt thou see above, Beatrice, thy blessed one! Smiling upon this mountain-top, her shalt thou see! Climb on!"

Thus as we climbed, we came upon a grassy valley where the Great Ones wait to enter in. With songs of praise, these spirits, singing, wait; and here the green is not the glittering green of cold enamel but the tender green of grass, with flowers of many colors all bedight, a scene of living tenderness and joy, and here the angels who descend, have garments green as leaflets just now born! Hence, in my sleep a saintly lady sweet did bear me up unto the very gate which pierces through the cliffs that circle Purgatory round. There on the steps an angel stood with flaming sword to keep the gate. Upon my forehead seven letters he made, to mind me of those sins which I must lose in climbing up the height within. Then did he open up the gate; and there no sooner did the door upon its hinges turn than like a thunderpeal I heard the sound of voices mingled in sweet melody. "We praise thee, Lord! We praise thee! Praise!" Ah me, how different are these entrance-sounds from the Infernal; for with anthems here one enters and below with wild laments.

What terraces above us rose, what steep ascents by stairways cut in rock! Yet as we climbed, the Sacred Stairs more easy seemed than they had looked to us when on the plain below we stood. "Thy feet will be so vanquished by good will," my master said, "that thou will climb not only knowing no fatigue but with delight!"

From terrace up to terrace mounted we, and on each one beheld those quiet shades that live in penitence and prayer, forever striving upward toward that Earthly Paradise of Joy that crowns the summit of the mount. Though bowed by pride or other sin unpurged, there ever came to them sweet visions bright of angels, vested all in white, with faces shining tremulous as doth the morning star. There heard they songs of those who sang: "Ah, blessed are the merciful! Blessed, the pure-in-heart!" and all those other Blesseds wherein the heavens rejoice. So upward ever strove they, upward always up; and we strove upward, too, until we came to that dread place where sprang a fire across our path, a sheet of flame that seemed to bar our way forever from Mt. Purgatory's top. In fear I started back; but once again my guide said in mine ear, "Beyond that flame she waits, she, Beatrice!" Then through these flames I leapt, though hotter they than molten glass! I climbed the last steep hard ascent and found myself within a heavenly wood, all dense and living green in morning light, a place serene and sweet with flowerets painted o'er. There all the soil breathed fragrance and a wind so gently blew it swayed the tree-tops lightly, till the rustle of their leaves bore sweet accompaniment to singing birds, that with full ravishment of joy did greet the new-sprung day! These words I heard, "The Good Supreme, sole in itself delighting, created man good, and gave to him this goodly place as promise of eternal peace!" And so I knew I was in Paradise.

Then saw I a procession come with candlesticks. "Hosanna!" sang they. Leaders saw I and a multitude of people clad in white, the Church triumphant, in its midst a chariot by a griffin drawn, and all surrounded by a group of maids, who went forever dancing at the wheel and showering flowers! Now in the bosom of this cloud of flowers, in snow-white veil and mantle green, above a gown of red, she came, whom I so longed to see, she, Beatrice, my Blessed One! Abashed I felt, so long a time had passed since I had seen her. Of that ancient love I felt again the power, the power sublime, that pierced me through ere from my boyhood I had yet come forth!

I turned to him, my guide, to say: "No drop of blood remains in me that does not tremble with the traces of this ancient flame!"

But he was gone, my master, Vergil! Who so far had led me, vanished here. No further could his cool philosophy lead on. To mount the heavenly heights, to soar unbound by earth, I needs must have as guide that one who could through love's keen urge awake my spirit to aspire and to attain the stars!

At first her eye was stern, "When thou through me hadst learned to love the highest good, why didst thou turn aside as soon as I was gone, and satisfy thyself with false delights?" she said.

But while with stern rebuke she spoke my name, the ice about my heart began to melt, as melts the snow on mountain heights, and in swift overflow came gushing from my lips in words of shame, the while I made confession of my wrong. Then smiled she, Beatrice. She bade me drink of two great rivers, whereby I should forget all evil and remember only good, and when from these most holy waters I returned, I was refreshed, renewed like trees renewed with leaves. Full ready was I then to mount unto the stars!

I gazed upon my guide, sweet Beatrice. Through realms of ether blue we soared aloft, forever up and up, while round about like iron from molten fire the sunlight sparkled, till I saw so much of heaven enkindled, that neither rain nor river ever made a lake so wide.

I wondered much that in this manner I could soar; but gazing on me with a pitying sigh, as mother on her child, did Beatrice explain: "Thou shouldst not marvel so. 'Tis no less natural for the soul to soar when from all burden of its sins 'tis free than for a rivulet to run from some high mount down to the plain below. More shouldst thou marvel if, thus freed, thou couldst still sit below and earthbound keep the living fire."

Thereat she heavenward turned her gaze. I kept my gaze on her; and longing for the Source of that great light did bear us up. Through all the Heavens we soared; from moon to stars, from stars to sun, from sun to stars again, and ever up and up, through eight effulgent worlds of light, eight worlds of light that ever brighter grew, all peopled with the spirits of the good.

"Hosanna, Holy God, illuming with thy brightness all the happy fires of these, thy realms!" So sang the spirits and in motion rapid, flew and ever flew, and moved as in a dance, till in the manner of swift-hurrying sparks with sudden distance, they did veil themselves.

In all these Heavens of bliss, what brightness we beheld, what glory, what rapidity of motion, music, melody, hosannas thundered as of organ peals. And as from star to star, from bliss to bliss, we passed, with ever greater joy smiled Beatrice, till with full splendor shone her laughing eyes. "Such light as this doth shine for all;" she said, "for God created man sincere and good. 'Tis sin alone which doth shut out the light and render him unlike the Good Supreme."

And when too great the splendors I beheld, sweet Beatrice did comfort me as doth a mother a bewildered child. O Beatrice, thou gentle Guide and dear! I kept my gaze on her, till more than once she said; "Why doth my face so much enamor thee? Look not at me but out upon the splendors round about!" And when the Seventh Heaven we had passed, she said: "Look down now and behold how vast a world thou hast already put beneath thy feet!"

I looked, and far below, beyond the seven spheres, I saw the earth so small, that I must smile to see it so ignoble there.

So soared we unto that Ninth Heaven which is pure light, pure light alone, diaphanous, transparent, crystalline. Here is the light of mind replete with love, and love of good replete with ecstasy. All moves with utter swiftness here, through the intensity of deep desire in every part to be conjoined with that bright light that from the Eternal Fountain rains above. So flashed the Living Light I scarce could bear its glory. In conformation then as of a snow-white rose, all flying through the air, appeared to me the saintly host whom Christ had saved, while therefrom rose and sank as bees into a flower, that heavenly host who mounting see and sing the glory of the Living Light. I turned to ask my lady of these wondrous things; but found, instead, an old man by my side, his eyes and cheeks o'erflowing with his joy. Sweet Beatrice was gone. My guide had left me there.

"She, where is she?" I cried. He pointed me to where she sat high up above me with angelic choirs upon their thrones.

"O lady, thou in whom my hope is strong," I cried; "and who for my salvation didst endure to leave in Hell the imprints of thy feet, thou from a slave hast brought me unto freedom, and may this soul of mine, which thou hast healed, pleasing to thee remain, till parted from the body I return to thee again!"

Thus I implored, and she, so far away, smiled, as it seemed, and looked once more at me; then unto the Eternal Fountain turned.

O grace abundant, by which thereafter I too dared to fix mine eyes upon the Light Eternal, Source of all the light on earth. I looked and I beheld—O Light Eterne, sole in thyself that dwelleth, sole knowest thyself and known unto thyself, who knowing, lovest, and smilest at thyself! In light which shone from Thee, I saw, as by reflection, something that I recognized as like to me, a man, and yet Thine image too, the likeness of Thy glory bright. How man could be the brightness of Thy glory and the shine of Thy great light, I wished to know; but mine own wings were not enough for this. There smote my mind a flash of lightning, and I knew at last, that deep within my heart and soul, what turned my whole desire and will was Thee, the Love which moves the Sun and all the Stars.

THE NEW COLOSSUS*
Emma Lazarus

Not like the brazen giant of Greek fame,
With conquering limbs astride from land to land;
Here at our sea-washed, sunset gates shall stand
A mighty woman with a torch, whose flame
Is the imprisoned lightning, and her name
Mother of Exiles. From her beacon-hand
Glows world-wide welcome; her mild eyes command
The air-bridged harbor that twin cities frame.
"Keep, ancient lands, your storied pomp!" cries she
With silent lips. "Give me your tired, your poor,
Your huddled masses yearning to breathe free,
The wretched refuse of your teeming shore.
Send these, the homeless, tempest-tost to me,
I lift my lamp beside the golden door!"

*From *Poems*. Used by permission of Houghton Mifflin Company.

The Melting Pot*
ISRAEL ZANGWILL

ON one of the giant ocean liners that ploughed its way through the broad Atlantic from Europe towards America, there crossed once a young Jewish lad from Russia. With hundreds of other Europeans, poor peasants mostly, in every sort of odd European costume and speaking every variety of odd European tongue, he was close packed in the rocking steerage of the boat. The berth in which he slept was scarcely wider than his fiddle case and it hung near the kitchen, where the hot rancid smell of food and the oil of the machinery made offensive odors all day long and all night long. But in spite of this, David Quixano was happy. He was going to America—America, the land of all his hopes! His whole life long he had dreamed of going to America. Everybody in Kishineff, the Russian city where he lived, had friends there, or got money orders from there, and the very earliest game he could ever remember playing was selling off his toy furniture and setting up in America.

If the journey sometimes seemed hard and long, he had only to pretend that he had been shipwrecked and that after clinging to a plank five days on the lonely Atlantic, his frozen form had been picked up by this great safe steamer, and then his poor little berth seemed delightful and the rancid food delicious. Some-

*Retold from the play by permission of The Macmillan Company.

times too he got out his beloved little old fiddle and played and played till he drew crowds of friendly faces about him. Somehow faces that turned towards David were always friendly, for there was that in the sunny warmth of his smile that left no room for aught but friendliness to answer it.

"A sunbeam took human shape when he was born," his uncle once had said.

And yet back in Russia David had left blackest memories. In the crowded Russian pale at Kishineff, wherein alone the Russian government permitted the Jews to dwell, he had once been the wonder-child who learned to play on the violin none knew how, out of his own heart, out of his own soul, with no other master; and old and young, rich and poor among the Jews had loved him. There dwelt his mother, too, and his father, and his sisters and his brothers, all happy together in the simple life of their little home. Then one day came into Kishineff a mysterious colonel in the uniform of the Tsar, and from him there began to ooze out into the city a secret poison of hatred against the Jews. Hatred and prejudice, calling itself religion, stirring the ugliest passions of men—first rumbling faintly like thunder in the distance, then swelling and roaring and gathering momentum till at last it burst in a hideous storm. Men and women in mobs, the scum of the town population, bore down on the unoffending dwellers in the pale, shouting, "Bey Zhida!" that is to say, "Kill the Jews!" Hither and thither they ran like tigers, looting, trampling peaceful men and women under foot, pitching children out of windows, stealing money, gold, silver, jewels, while the police and military officials lifted not a finger to protect the helpless or to stay the dastardly crime. Before David's very eyes father, mother, sisters, brothers fell, down to the youngest babe, while that mysterious colonel in the uniform of the Tsar stood by with cold aloofness, giving orders and looking on. David himself but escaped with his life because he was shot in the shoulder and fell to the ground unconscious, so the murderers left him for dead.

Ah! David was a sunny lad indeed, but when he thought back on what had happened to him in Russia, all the world for him was twisted out of shape; he saw it all through a fiery red mist; grief and anger filled his soul and he shrieked out against that butcher's face, shrieked out as though in all his life was but one wish—to find the owner of that face and make him pay the penalty for his crime. At such times he would get down his beloved fiddle and play and play and play. At first his violin would send forth crashing discords like the discord in his soul, but always at last his music fell into the sweet concord of perfect harmony with all the notes blending in unison. Then gradually the red mist would disappear and David be himself again.

At length the great steamer drew into New York Harbor. A little tug came out to meet it, leaving behind a smudgy trail of smoke, and as the small boat bobbed up and down on the choppy waves just beside the great one, a pilot made a perilous ascent by a swinging ladder up the side of the liner to the deck. All round about were hundreds of other tugs and launches, great boats and little boats from every quarter of the world, with funnels painted all different colors and flags of every nation fluttering in the breeze. But best of all to David, as he stood close to the rail looking out on it all with a fast-beating heart, were the American flags he saw everywhere—the stars and stripes, emblem of the America of his dreams, the America where were forever impossible the horrors of Kishineff.

Soon the shore-line of lower New York appeared, its giant sky-scrapers at tremendous heights cleaving the blue of the sky, but as the sea-weary passengers crowded to the rail, that which beckoned them first, that which bade them tenderly welcome as to a land of promise, was the colossal Statue of Liberty rising out of the harbor. In the midst of Jew and Gentile, Russian and Pole, Greek and Italian, Armenian and Turk, German and

Hungarian, Norwegian and Swede, there stood David, and before these wanderers from Europe who had turned their backs on the old world and their faces toward the new, loomed up out of the shining blue waters, that great gilded statue, lifting high her torch to lighten all the world.

Some among those immigrants tossed their caps in the air and cheered, some laughed and sang, some turned soon to other things, but some, like David, kept their eyes fixed in that one direction, moved almost to tears. Back of them lay who knew what of suffering, injustice and crushing poverty, but before them lay the land of hope, of equal rights and opportunities. To David that gigantic torch lifted high above the world a great ideal of liberty and justice, equal rights for Jew and Gentile, rich and poor, black and white, an ideal which should some day draw all men up to it in one grand brotherhood. That was the dream that had led him there, led him forth out of blood-soaked Kishineff to the shores of the Land of Promise. And so, clasping tight in his arms his beloved fiddle in its shabby case, he watched with solemn joy.

His joyousness did not desert him even during the trying time when, like herded cattle, he and the other immigrants were put off at Ellis Island and marshaled and driven through all the series of rigid examinations with which our United States welcomes newcomers to her shores. No, David had no complaints to make. He loved it all. He could not even speak the language of America and yet he was not lonely; the language of its spirit spoke surely to his heart and made him feel at home.

At length the day came when there he was in New York itself, and there was his good uncle, Mendel Quixano, to meet him, and his dear old grandmother, too, a venerable figure in the prescribed black wig of the orthodox Jewess, clasping him in her arms and half sobbing his name in Yiddish, "Dovidel! Dovidel! Dovidel!"

Ah! but the home where his uncle and grandmother lived in New York seemed fine to him after the garret from which he had come in Russia and his tiny cramped quarters on the boat. It was an old house having a veranda with pillars in the colonial style, and on the door was carefully nailed a Mezuzah, a tiny metal case containing a passage from the Bible which every good Jew was commanded to have fastened to his doorpost. In the comfortable living room cheap chairs stood next a grand piano piled with music; huge mouldering old Hebrew tomes assorted with modern English books; and on the walls pictures of Wagner,

Columbus, Washington, and Lincoln had to make themselves at home beside the Mizrach, or sacred Jewish picture hanging ever on the east wall toward Jerusalem. The whole effect was a curious blend of shabbiness, Americanism, Jewishness and music, all four of which seemed combined in the figure of Mendel Quixano, an elderly music master with a fine Jewish face pathetically furrowed by misfortune and graced by a short grizzled beard.

"A shabby place enough," Mendel would often say, looking discontentedly about. But David always made answer, "What's the matter with this room? It's princely. If it were only on board a boat not the richest man in America could afford such a magnificent cabin!"

In truth Mendel Quixano had been somewhat soured by misfortunes and disappointments, and he had by no means the sunny nature of David. With big hopes of becoming a great musician he had come to America, only to find that in order to pay the rent and support himself and his mother he must give music lessons every day in the week to little "brainless, earless, thumb-fingered Gentiles!" When his whole soul longed for the best in music, he must play cheap waltzes and rag-time for dances, at theatres, and in music halls.

"Ach Gott! What a life! What a life!" he would often sigh.

Mendel did not see in America what David did. He saw that there was still much prejudice here against his race, still much injustice, greed and inequality among men. His thoughts were only half turned forward toward the new world; half they were still turned back towards the past, toward the sad history of the Jews and the wrongs they had suffered at the hands of the Gentiles all down through the ages. And the old grandmother who loved David so dearly, she who had lost her whole family save David and Mendel in Europe, she was wrapped up in thinking of the past, in observing the rites and ceremonies of her religion as her father had done and her father's father before her. Life

was sad and lonely for her in America where she had no friends
and understood nothing of the language, for never in all the ten
years since Mendel had brought her there, had she dropped her
Yiddish or learned to speak a single word of English.

Loving and considerate of the dear old grandmother was
David, patient with all her little peculiarities and demands,
affectionate and obedient to his uncle Mendel, yet his own face
was always turned with joyous confidence toward the present and
the future, away from the dead and vanished past. True, as
time went on, he, too, perceived that in America men were greedy
still, dishonest, selfish, unjust, that thither came many a one
who thought that liberty meant the freedom to do as he chose,
instead of the freedom to do as he ought. Yet in spite of it all,
he kept his faith firm and strong in the America of his dreams—
that America which he came to see existed yet as an idea only,
but an idea that would surely compel men into line with it, one
day govern them wholly, and so reveal itself as the only true
America there ever was or ever could be.

With this unseen yet real America David kept his faith and he
gradually came to express all that he thought and felt about it in
a great piece of music, his American symphony. Yet he was only
a poor musician playing as Mendel did, in theatres and cheap dance
halls. How was he ever to get his symphony, into which he had
put his whole heart and soul, played by a great orchestra before
the public? It was the dream of his life to hear it actually coming
out of violins and cellos, drums and trumpets, thundering its message to America and all the world. But how was he to get it done,
—how? Mendel did not understand the symphony and only half
believed it to be great. It must, he was sure, be full of faults, since
David was so young, so inexperienced, and had never had a teacher
for even the simplest rules of harmony. Yet Mendel was proud
of his nephew and he believed that if only David could be sent
to Germany to study, he might perhaps really produce something

great. But how was even this to be accomplished when they were so poor and scarcely now made both ends meet?

One day David played, as he often did, without pay, at a charitable entertainment in a great Settlement House that lent its aid to hundreds of immigrants just such as he had once been. Thither came Dutchmen and Frenchmen, Italians and Greeks, Norwegians and Swedes, still in outlandish garments, still jabbering in outlandish tongues, with little, round, brown-eyed children and little, round, blue-eyed children, all meeting together on the grounds of a few broken words of English. And how they listened and soaked in David's music! How they cheered and whistled and applauded! At the Settlement David met Miss Vera Revendal, who was one of the workers there. Vera loved music as dearly as David and was interested at once in his playing.

Though David never dreamed it, Vera was Russian and had been born in that same Kishineff so connected for him with hideous memories overtopped by the "butcher's face." Her father was a member of the nobility and a faithful follower of the Tsar, sharing all the contempt of the Russian aristocrats for the lower classes and their hatred and prejudice against the Jews. Yet Vera, even as a little school girl, had seen with a heart overflowing with compassion, what misery and poverty was wrought among the Russian people by the tyranny of the Tsar. What rights to liberty and happiness had the lower classes in Russia? None! None! None! All Russia existed for the pleasure of the nobles and the Tsar. With a fearless, uncompromising childish demand for justice Vera refused all respect or reverence for the Tsar. Once when she was in attendance at the Imperial High School, the Tsar had come thither to pay an annual visit. As was his custom he tasted the food that was served the children, and the high and mighty honor of finishing what he left was reserved for the show pupil from among all the classes. On Vera this honor fell, but when the plate of mutton, sanctified by the royal touch, was set before her, she horrified all the expectant circle about by passionately pushing it from her and passing it off to be consumed by the poorest among the servants! That was the sort of girl young Vera was, and though she had loved her father dearly, the Baron Revendal, honest but bigoted, clung obstinately to his class and the service of the Tsar. So when Vera was arrested as a revolutionist, attempting to overthrow the government of tyranny in Russia, he had turned his back on his mother-

less daughter. Vera was sentenced to exile in desolate Siberia and thither she would have been sent had she not escaped from her gaolers and made her way to America where she found her life work among the poor in the Settlements of New York.

Of all this David knew nothing, and no more did Vera know or dream that David was a Jew. The two found simple pleasure in their mutual love of music. A short time after David's first appearance at the Settlement an invitation was sent him to play for them once more, and Vera went herself one bright winter's afternoon to seek him out and get his consent in person.

On that particular day David was from home, and Mendel Quixano, in a seedy velvet jacket, had been giving a music lesson. Suddenly from the kitchen came the noise of an irate Irish voice and the shrill Yiddish of an angry Frau Quixano.

"Divil take the butther!" cried Kathleen, the Irish servant. "I wouldn't put up wid yez, not for a hundred dollars a week!"

"*Wos shreist du?*" shrilled Frau Quixano. "*Gott in Himmel! dieses Amerika.*" Mendel heaved a deep sigh. "Ach! Mother and Kathleen at it again!" he muttered. It seemed to him that one's very servants in America hated the Jews.

"Pots and pans and plates and knives!" went on Kathleen still in the kitchen. "Sure, 'tis enough to make a saint chrazy!" And she burst into the living room clutching a white table cloth. "Bad luck to me if iver I take sarvice again with haythen Jews!" Just then she perceived Mendel huddled up in the arm chair by the fire, and gave a little scream. "Och! I thought ye was out!"

"She said I put mate on a butther plate," Kathleen protested.

"Well, you know that's against her religion," answered Mendel.

"But I didn't do nothing of the sort! I only put butther on a mate plate."

"That's just as bad. The Bible forbids both butter and meat—"

"Sure! who can rimimber all that?" Kathleen began venting her spite on the litter of things she was vigorously clearing off the table. "Why don't ye have a sinsible religion?"

"You are impertinent!" Mendel seated himself at the piano and began to play softly. "Attend to your work."

"And isn't it layin' the Sabbath cloth I am?"

"Don't answer me back!"

"Faith! I must answer *somebody* back and sorra a word of English *she* understands. I might as well talk to a tree! What way can I be understandin' her jabberin' and jibberin'? I'm not a monkey. Why don't she talk English like a Christian?"

"You are not paid to talk but work!" said Mendel.

"And who *can* work wid an ould woman nagglin' and grizzlin' and faultin' me? Mate plates, butther plates, *kosher, trepha!* Sure, I've smashed up folks' crockery and they makin' less fuss about it!"

Mendel stopped playing. "Breaking crockery is one thing and breaking a religion another," said he. "Didn't you tell me when I engaged you that you had lived in other Jewish families?"

"And is it a liar ye'd make me out now?" cried Kathleen angrily. "I've lived wid clothiers and pawnbrokers and vaudeville actors, but I niver shtruck a house where mate and butther couldn't be as paceable on the same plate as eggs and bacon! Faith, ye can keep yer dirthy wages. I give ye notice! I'll quit off this blissid minute!"

And she dumped down a silver candlestick and rushed hysterically off to her room. Just then there came a rat-a-tat-tat at the street door.

"Kathleen!" Mendel hurried to the door of the irate maiden's room. "There's a visitor!"

"I'm not here," called Kathleen angrily from within.

"So long as you are in this house, you must do your work," ordered Mendel.

"I tould ye I was lavin' at once. Let ye open the door yerself."

"But I'm not dressed to receive visitors. It may be a new pupil." And off went Mendel, leaving Kathleen naught to do but obey.

"The divil fly away wid me if iver from this hour I set foot again among haythen furriners," muttered Kathleen, emerging from her stronghold and crossing unwillingly to the door. As she opened it Vera appeared in the vestibule, her beautiful face glowing forth from a setting of snowy furs.

"Is Mr. Quixano at home?" asked Vera.

"Which Mr. Quixano?" queried Kathleen sulkily.

"The one who plays," answered Vera.

"There isn't a 'one' who plays." Kathleen's voice was fairly snappy. "Yer wrong entirely. They both plays."

"Oh dear," smiled Vera. "Then it's the one who plays the violin—Mr. David—I want to see."

"He's out!" Kathleen made a move to slam the door.

"Don't shut the door," cried Vera. "I want to leave a message."

"Then why don't ye come inside? It's freezin' me ye are!"

And Kathleen sneezed a loud and accusing "Atchoo!"

"I'm sorry," Vera entered the room. "Will you please tell Mr. Quixano that Miss Revendal called from the Settlement and—"

"What way will I be tellin' him all that?" bridled Kathleen. "I'm not here!"

"Not here!" cried Vera.

"I'm lavin' as soon as I've me thrunk packed."

"Then may I write the message at this desk?"

"If the ould woman don't come in and shpy you!"

"Who is she?" asked Vera.

"Ould Mr. Quixano's mother. She wears a black wig, she's that houly."

Vera was bewildered. "But why should she mind my writing?"

"Look at the clock," Kathleen drew her face into an expression of comical solemnity. "If ye're not quick, it'll be *Shabbos* and Lord forbid any work should be done in this house on *Shabbos*."

"Be what?" cried Vera.

Kathleen held up her hands in horror. "Ye don't know what *Shabbos* is? A Jewess not know her own Sunday!"

Vera froze on the instant. After all, the prejudice of the most aristocratic blood in Russia was not wholly blotted out in her. She felt outraged that anyone should mistake her for a Jewess.

"I a Jewess! How dare you!" she cried. "I am a Russian!" Then she added slowly, as if half dazed, "Do I understand that Mr. Quixano is a Jew?"

"Two Jews, Miss," answered Kathleen, "both of 'em."

"Oh, but it is impossible," murmured Vera. "He had such charming manners. Are you sure Mr. Quixano is not Spanish?"

"Shpanish!" Kathleen picked up an old Hebrew book on the arm chair. "Look at the ould lady's book. Is that Shpanish?" And she pointed to the Mizrach on the wall. "And that houly picture, is that Shpanish?"

Convinced against her will that David was a Jew, Vera suddenly changed her mind about leaving him a message. "Don't say I called at all," said she. But just at that moment Mendel Quixano appeared in the room, completely transformed in his neat Prince Albert coat, and Vera could not escape. When he learned it was David whom she had come to see, he invited her in so gentlemanly a manner to wait that she struggled with her prejudice, overcame it, and sat down.

"That wonderful boy a Jew," she kept saying to herself. "But then so was David the shepherd youth with his harp and his psalms, the sweet singer in Israel."

While she waited conversing with Mendel, Frau Quixano came into the room with excited gesticulations, chattering in Yiddish angry complaints against Kathleen. Perceiving her precious Hebrew book on the floor where Kathleen had dropped it, she cried out in horror, picked it up and kissed it piously.

"*Ruhig, Mutter, ruhig!*" Mendel pressed her soothingly into her fireside chair, then he added to Vera. "She understands barely a word of English."

Frau Quixano eyed the newcomer suspiciously.

"Tell her I hope she is well," said Vera.

Mendel translated the young woman's words into Yiddish but Frau Quixano only shrugged her shoulders and said in despairing astonishment. "*Gut? Un'wie soll es gut gehen—in Amerika?*"

"She asks how can anything possibly go well in America." Mendel explained.

"Ah!" said Vera, "then your mother does not like America!"

Mendel half smiled. "Her favorite exclamation is '*A Klog zu Columbussen!*' that is, 'Cursed be Columbus!'"

Vera laughed as the old woman settled herself to read. "But your nephew, he does not curse America?" she said.

"David—ah, no! He is crazy about America. My mother came here with her life behind her, David with his life before him!" Mendel paused for a moment, then he went on gloomily, "But what is there here for him, poor boy? Only a terrible struggle for existence—music halls and dance halls, beer halls and weddings. Every hope and ambition will be ground out of him and he will die obscure and unknown." The musician's head sank sadly on his breast and Frau Quixano began to sob faintly over her book.

"There," said Vera, "you have made your mother cry."

"Oh, no," said Mendel, "she understood nothing. She always cries on the eve of Sabbath. She knows that in this great grinding America David and I must go out to work on Sabbath as on week days. She never says a word to us but her heart is full of tears."

"Poor old woman," said Vera.

For a time nothing was heard in the room save the low sobbing of Frau Quixano and the roar of the wind. With the slowly gathering dusk there seemed to droop over all a lurking pall of sadness. Then suddenly a happy voice was heard outside singing:

> "*My country, 'tis of thee,*
> *Sweet land of liberty,*
> *Of thee I sing.*"

Frau Quixano pricked up her ears. "Do ist Dovidel!" she cried.

The whole atmosphere seemed changed at once from grief to joy as David opened the door and appeared on the threshold, a buoyant, snow covered figure carrying a violin case and clad in a cloak and a broad-brimmed hat.

"Isn't it a beautiful world, uncle," he cried, "snow, the divine white snow!" Then perceiving the visitor, he removed his hat and looked at her with boyish reverence and wonder.

IN SHINING ARMOR

"Miss Revendal here!" he cried. "If I had only known you were waiting."

"Don't look so surprised," said Vera, smiling. "I haven't fallen from heaven like the snow. I'm glad you didn't know I was waiting. Your uncle told me you were playing at the Crippled Children's Home. I wouldn't have cheated those little ones of a moment of your music."

"Ah! it was bully! You should have seen the cripples waltzing with their crutches! Even the paralyzed danced. If they hadn't the use of their legs, their arms danced on the counterpane! If their arms couldn't dance, their hands danced, if their hands couldn't dance, their heads danced, if their heads couldn't dance —why, their eyes danced! Dear little cripples! I felt as though I could play them all straight again with the love and joy jumping out of this old fiddle! *Es war grossartig*, Granny!" And David moved toward the old grandmother by the fire, patting her cheek in greeting while she responded with a loving smile ere she settled herself to slumber contentedly over her book. When David learned that Vera had come to ask him to play once more at the Settlement he was overjoyed.

"But we can't offer you a fee," said Vera.

"A fee!" cried David. "I'd pay a fee to see all your happy immigrants. It's almost as good as going to Ellis Island."

"What a strange taste." Vera smiled. "Who on earth wants to go to Ellis Island?"

"Oh," David's face beamed, "I love going to Ellis Island to watch the ships coming in from Europe and to think that all those weary, sea tossed wanderers are feeling what I felt when America first stretched out her great mother-hand to *me*."

"You were very happy?" asked Vera softly.

"Happy? It was heaven. You must remember that all my life America was waiting for me, beckoning, shining—the place where God would wipe away tears from off all faces." His voice ended with a queer little catch in his breath that always proclaimed his thoughts had gone back to Kishineff. Mendel rose and went to him half frightened.

"Now, now, David, don't get excited," he said. But David paid no heed.

"To think that the same great torch of liberty which threw its light across all the broad seas and lands into my little garret in Russia, is shining also for all those other weeping millions of Europe, shining wherever men hunger and are oppressed."

"Yes, yes, David." Mendel laid his hand soothingly on his shoulder. "Now sit down and—"

"Shining over the starving villages of Italy and Ireland, over the swarming stony cities of Poland and Galicia, over the ruined farms of Roumania, over the shambles of Russia. Oh, Miss Revendal,—" David's voice was choking now with the depths of his feeling, "when I look at our Statue of Liberty I just seem to hear the voice of America crying: 'Come unto me, all ye that labor and are heavy laden, and I will give you rest—rest—'"

"Don't talk any more now, David." Mendel's voice had taken a tone of command. "You can express all this that you feel in your American Symphony."

"Ah, you compose music," cried Vera eagerly, for it was the first time she had known that David did more than play. "And you find inspiration for your composing in America?"

"Yes," David grew calm again. "I find inspiration in the seething of the crucible."

"The crucible!" cried Vera. "I do not understand."

"Not understand,—you the spirit of the Settlement! Not understand that America is God's crucible, the great Melting Pot, where all the races of Europe are melting and re-forming. Here you stand, good folk, think I, when I see them at Ellis Island, in your fifty groups with your fifty blood hatreds and rivalries. But you won't be long like that, brothers, for these are

the fires of God you've come to—these are the fires of God. A fig for your feuds and vendettas! Germans and Frenchmen, Irishmen and Englishmen, Jews and Russians, into the crucible with you all! God is making the American!"

"I should have thought the American was made already," said Mendel, "eighty millions of him."

"Eighty millions," cried David in good humored derision. "No, uncle, the real American has not yet arrived. He is only in the crucible, I tell you—he will be the fusion of all races, perhaps the coming superman! Ah! what a glorious ending for my symphony if I can only write it!"

Somehow Vera understood David better than his uncle or anyone else had ever done—David knew it; he felt it. Those others saw America as a certain wide stretch of land bounded by the Atlantic and Pacific; they saw the American as the man whom they daily met in the streets with his good points and his bad. But

Vera understood David's vision of America as a great ideal of liberty, humanity, and justice, and the real American as he who should some day express that ideal, representing in himself the melting together of all that was best and highest in the races of the world, purified from their old differences, their old false systems, their old hatreds and prejudices, their old suspicions and deceits.

"Won't you give a bit of your symphony at our concert?" asked Vera eagerly.

"Oh, it needs an orchestra!" David was once again shy.

"But you at the violin and I at the piano."

"Ah, you didn't tell me you played, Miss Revendal," interrupted Mendel.

"I told you less commonplace things," smiled Vera. "Yes, I studied at Petersburg. There wasn't much music at Kishineff—"

"Kishineff!" On the instant David was trembling.

"Yes," said Vera, "my birthplace!"

"So," David shuddered violently. "You are a Russian."

"Calm yourself, David." Mendel came protectingly toward him.

"Not much music at Kishineff!" David laughed strangely. "No! only the Death March. Mother! Father! Ah! cowards, murderers! And you!" He shook his fist in the air. "You looking on with your cold butcher's face! O God! O God!" And he ran shamefacedly out of the room.

"What have I done?" cried Vera.

Frau Quixano, who had fallen asleep over her book, awoke suddenly as if with a sense of horror and gazed dazedly about.

"*Dovidel! Wu ist Dovidel? Mir dacht sach—*"

Mendel pressed her back to her slumbers.

"*Du träumst, Mutter! Schlaf!*"

"His parents were massacred?" whispered Vera hoarsely.

"Yes! Before his very eyes," answered Mendel, sadly.

"Terrible!" cried Vera, "Terrible."

Mendel shrugged his shoulders. "It is only Jewish history."

IN SHINING ARMOR

Gone now was Vera's prejudice against David. On the contrary, her interest in the young musician had increased to such an extent that she offered to do her best to interest someone in him, someone rich enough to send him to Germany to study, and Mendel who would have been too proud to accept from a Gentile aught for himself, was grateful, almost ready to beg such a favor for David. Scarcely had she left the house when David came back into the room, once more composed, though somewhat dazed.

"She is gone?" he asked. "Oh, but I have driven her away by my craziness. But she understood, Uncle. She understood my crucible of God. You don't know what it means to me to have someone who understands. Even you have never understood—"

"Nonsense." Mendel was wounded. "How can Miss Revendal understand you better than your own uncle? What true understanding can there ever be between a Russian Jew and a Russian Christian?"

"What understanding?" cried David. "Why, aren't we both Americans?" Mendel shrugged his shoulders drily as he went out through the street door.

Once left to himself David set eagerly to work writing down on his musical manuscript all that had come to him as he talked with Vera, but he had worked only a few moments when Frau Quixano yawned, awakened and stretched herself, then looked at the clock.

"*Shabbos!*" she said and, rising, she lit the candlesticks on the table with a muttered Hebrew benediction. Crossing over to David, as he sat absorbed in his work, she touched him on the shoulder to remind him that he must stop his writing on *Shabbos*.

"Dovidel," he looked up dazedly while she pointed to the candles. "*Shabbos!*"

A sweet smile came over David's face. To him religion meant less a matter of rites and ceremonies than of a pure and contrite heart, nevertheless he threw the quill resignedly away and submitted his head to her hands and her ancient Hebrew blessing.

As she left the room, she shook her finger at him warningly lest he should go back to work again. *"Gut Shabbos,"* she said. David smiled after her. *"Gut Shabbos!"* he answered.

A moment later he was ready in his coat and hat to go out and give a music lesson. He was almost at the door when Kathleen came bustling into the room, fully dressed in outdoor garments and laden with an umbrella and a large brown paper parcel.

"Why Kathleen, you're not going out this bitter weather," said David.

"And who's to shtay me?" bridled Kathleen, sharply fending him off with her umbrella as he offered to relieve her of her parcel.

"Oh, but you mustn't! I'll do your errand for you. What is it?"

"Errand is it indeed!" cried Kathleen indignantly. "I'm not here!"

"Not here?" questioned David in surprise.

"I'm lavin'. They'll come for me thrunk."

"But who's sending you away?"

"It's sending meself I am. Yer houly grandmother has me disthroyed intirely."

"Why, what has the poor old lady—"

"I don't be saltin' the mate and I do be mixin' the crockery—"

"I know, I know," David spoke gently, "but Kathleen, remember, she was brought up to these things from her childhood. And her father was a Rabbi."

"What's that?" demanded Kathleen, "a priest?"

"A sort of a priest. In Russia he was a great man. Her husband too was a mighty scholar and to give him time to study holy books, she had to do chores all day for him and the children. But he died and the children left her—went to America and other far-off places or to heaven, and she was left penniless and alone."

"Poor ould lady!"

"Not so old yet! She was married at fifteen!"

"Poor young craythur!"

"But she was still the good angel of the congregation, sat up with the sick and watched over the dead."

"Saints alive!"

"And then one day my uncle sent the old lady a ticket to come to America. But it is not so happy for her here, because you see my uncle has to be near his theatre and can't live in the Jewish quarter, and so nobody understands her, and she sits all day alone, alone with her books and her religion and her memories."

"Oh, Mr. David!" Kathleen was breaking down.

"And now all this long, cold, snowy evening she'll sit by the fire alone thinking of her dead, and the fire will sink lower and lower, and she won't be able to touch it because it's the holy Sabbath, and there'll be no kind Kathleen to brighten up the grey ashes. And then at last, sad and shivering, she'll creep up to her room, and there in the dark and the cold—"

Kathleen burst into tears, dropped her parcel on the floor and tore her bonnet strings open.

"Oh, Mr. David, I won't mix the crockery. I won't!"

"Of course you won't," David spoke heartily. And off he went while Kathleen fell down before the fire and began to poke it strenuously, the best in her heart called forth by David's appeal to her sympathies. Jew or Gentile, what mattered it? In America all old-time enemies looked into each other's hearts and understood one another on the grounds of a common humanity.

Vera was as good as her word in seeking out someone who might be persuaded to send David to Europe, but among all her acquaintances the only one of great wealth in whom she could arouse the smallest interest was a certain young Quincy Davenport, and he was interested in David solely because he loved Vera and wished most particularly to please her. Quincy was one of those young Americans who had never done any useful work in all his life, but spent his days finding new and exciting ways in which to spend the enormous income that came to him from his father. The greater part of his time he passed in Europe and the rest in trying to ape European manners and customs and introduce them into America. Lazy, idle, pretentious, he saw in America only a crude sort of place, good for nothing much except as a spot where his father could make heaps of American dollars for his son to spend on thrilling amusements and pleasures.

Scarcely a month after Vera had first promised Mendel to find someone to help David, she sent him word that she was bringing Mr. Davenport and Herr Pappelmeister, the conductor of Mr. Davenport's private orchestra, to see the young man, and that if Herr Pappelmeister found in the music he had written any evidence of genius, the symphony would be produced in Mr. Davenport's wonderful marble music hall before five hundred of the most fashionable folk in America, and David would be sent to Europe. Mendel was aglow with hope. How much it meant—this coming of Quincy Davenport, yet he could hardly interest David at all in the matter. The young man scarcely even listened to his uncle's information. His head was full of the great ending he was writing to his symphony. He had just seen a thousand little foreign born children saluting the Stars and Stripes, and the sight had filled his soul with all he wanted to finish his work.

"Just fancy it, uncle!" he cried. "The Stars and Stripes unfurled, and a thousand childish voices, piping and foreign, fresh from the lands of oppression, hailing its fluttering folds. Ah! but if you had heard them—'Flag of our Great Republic'— the words have gone singing at my heart ever since—'Flag of our

Great Republic, Guardian of our homes, whose stars and stripes stand for Bravery, Purity, Truth and Union, we salute thee. We, the natives of distant lands who find rest under thy folds, do pledge our hearts, our lives, our sacred honor, to love and protect thee, our Country, and the liberty of the American people forever.'"

"Quite right," said Mendel, who had been vainly trying to turn David's thoughts toward his own life and the great chance now before him. "But you needn't get so excited over it."

"Not get excited when one hears the roaring of the fires of God? When one sees souls melting in the Crucible? Uncle, all those little immigrants will grow up Americans!"

"But, David," cried Mendel. "Surely some day you'd like your music produced—you'd like it to go all over the world?"

"Wouldn't it be glorious—all over the world and down the ages!"

"But don't you see that unless you go and study seriously in Germany?—" Just at that moment in came Kathleen from the kitchen, carrying a tea tray with ear-shaped cakes and bread and butter for the expected guests, and wearing a grotesque false nose.

"Kathleen!" cried Mendel in amaze, but David burst out into boyish laughter.

"Sure, what's the matter?" cried Kathleen standing still with her tray.

"Look into the glass!" laughed David.

Kathleen crossed to the mantel. "Houly Moses." She dropped the tray so quickly as she snatched off the false nose that it would all have gone to smash had not Mendel, fortunately, caught it. "Och, I forgot to take it off—'twas the misthress gave it me —I put it on to cheer her up."

"Is she so miserable then, the grandmother?" asked David.

"Terrible low, Mr. David, today bein' Purim."

Kathleen's voice was as sympathetic as though she had never been otherwise than most kindly disposed toward her mistress.

"But Purim is a merry time for us, Kathleen, like our carnival," said David.

"That's what the misthress is so miserable about. Ye don't *keep* carnival. There's noses for both of ye in the kitchen—didn't I go with her to Hester Street to buy 'em?—but ye don't be axin for 'em. And to see your noses layin' around so solemn and neglected, faith, it nearly makes me chry meself."

"Who can remember about Purim in America?" said Mendel bitterly, but David only smiled. "Poor granny, tell her to come in and I'll play her a Purim jig."

"No, no, David," interrupted Mendel hastily. "Not here—the visitors!"

"Visitors!" cried David. "What visitors?"

Mendel grew impatient. "That's just what I've been trying to explain."

"Well, I can play in the kitchen, then!" And off went David with his violin while Mendel shrugged his shoulders hopelessly at the boy's perversity. Soon from the kitchen was heard the sound of a merry Slavic jig with Frau Quixano laughing and calling Kathleen to join in the fun. Even Mendel's feet began to keep time to the music, when the hoot of an automobile and the rattling of a car warned him that the guests were come. In another moment Vera and Quincy appeared in the room. Quincy was adorned with an orchid and eye-glass and was quite evidently a dude. It was equally evident, too, that he deeply admired Miss Revendal. There followed soon after them Herr Pappelmeister, a burly German with a leonine head, enormous spectacles, and a mane of white hair. He appeared very grave and silent and clutched a bunchy umbrella of which he never let go. Herr Pappelmeister was a famous musical conductor, who enjoyed a salary of twenty thousand dollars a year conducting Quincy's private orchestra for the amusement of Quincy's friends. Quincy himself had no knowledge of music, but he had brought Herr Pappelmeister to discover if David had any real genius.

"I'm so sorry," said Mendel to Vera. "I can't get David to come into the room. He's terribly shy."

"Won't face the music, eh?" sniggered Quincy.

"Did you tell him *I* was here?" questioned Vera, disappointed.

"Of course!" answered Mendel. "He will not come. But I've persuaded him to let me show you his manuscript." Then he turned anxiously to Pappelmeister. "You must remember his youth and his lack of musical education."

"Blease, the manusgribt," said Pappelmeister.

Mendel moved David's music stand into the center of the room and Pappelmeister put the manuscript on it. "So!" All eyes centered eagerly on him. With irritating elaborateness he polished his glasses and then read in silence.

"But!" cried Quincy, bored by the silence. "Won't you play it?"

"Blay it?" cried Pappelmeister. "Am I an orgestra? I blay it in my brain." And he went on reading, ruffling his hair unconsciously,—"So!"

"You don't seem to like it," said Vera anxiously.

"I do not comprehend it."

"I knew it was crazy," said Mendel. "It is supposed to be about America or a crucible or something. And of course there are heaps of mistakes."

Pappelmeister became absorbed again in the music, sublimely unconscious of all about him. "Ach, so—so,—So! Dot is some-dings different!" He began to beat time with his ridiculous bunchy umbrella, moving more and more vigorously till at last he was conducting elaborately as if a whole orchestra sat before him, stretching out his left palm for pianissimo passages and raising it vigorously for forte with every now and then an exclama-tion. "*Wunderschön!* Now the flutes! Clarinets! Ach *ergötzlich* —bassoons and drums. *Kolossal! Kolossal!*"

"Bravo! Bravo!" Vera clapped her hands. "I'm so excited."

"Then it isn't bad, Poppy?" yawned Quincy.

"Sh! Sh! Piano!" Pappelmeister was not even listening.

"Don't say Sh! to me!" cried Quincy outraged. "Look here, Poppy," and he seized the wildly waving umbrella. "We can't be here all day."

With a blank stare Pappelmeister returned to himself.

"Ach! What it is?" he cried.

"What it is!—we've had enough!" said Quincy.

"Enough? Of such a beaudiful symphony?"

"It may be beautiful to you," said Quincy. "But it's blamed stupid for us! See here, Poppy, if you're satisfied that the young fellow has sufficient talent to be sent to study in Germany—"

"Germany!" interrupted Herr Pappelmeister. "Germany has nodings to teach him. He has to teach Germany."

"Bravo!" cried Vera again.

"I always said he was a genius!" said Mendel.

"Then his stuff can go on one of my programs?" asked Quincy.

"I should be broud to indroduce it to de vorld."

At that joyous news Mendel hastened to the kitchen and fairly dragged David into the room.

"Oh, Mr. Quixano, I'm so glad," cried Vera. "Mr. Davenport is going to produce your symphony in his wonderful marble music room."

"Yes, young man," said Quincy, "I'm going to give you the most fashionable audience in America, and if Poppy is right, you are just going to rake in the dollars."

For one long moment David spoke not a word in answer to this magnificent offer. Was he trying to realize the good fortune that lay at his feet? All at once he drew himself up in a peculiar manner, then he turned to Vera and said: "I can never be grateful enough to you, and I can never be grateful enough to Herr Pappelmeister. It is an honor even to meet him."

"Mein brave young man!" cried Pappelmeister, choked with emotion and patting him on the back.

"But before I accept Mr. Davenport's kindness, I must know to whom I am indebted." His voice grew suddenly stern and he looked Quincy full in the eyes. "Is it true that you live in America only two months of the year and then only to entertain Europeans who wander to these wild parts?"

"Lucky for you, young man," said Quincy, toying with his eye-glass. "You'll have an Italian prince and a British duke to hear your scribblings."

"And the palace where they will hear my scribblings. Is it true that—?"

"Mr. Quixano," interrupted Vera on pins and needles lest he spoil his chance—"what possible—?" but David entreatingly held up his hand for silence and went on with an increase of firm self-command:

"Is this palace the same whose grounds were turned into Venetian canals where the guests ate in gondolas, gondolas that were draped with the most wonderful trailing silks in imitation of the Venetian nobility in their great winter fêtes?"

"Ah, Miss Revendal," Quincy turned to Vera. "What a pity you refused that invitation. It was a fairy scene of twinkling lights and delicious darkness. Each couple supped in their own gondola—"

"And the same night men and women died of hunger in New York!" David delivered his words with stinging directness, like a blow that came straight from the shoulder.

"What!" Quincy was so startled he dropped his eye-glass.

"And this is the sort of people you would invite to hear my symphony—these gondola-guzzlers!"

"Mr. Quixano!" cried Vera.

"David!" cried Mendel.

"You low down ungrateful—!" yelled Quincy.

"Not for you and such as you have I sat here writing and dreaming,—not for you shall my music sing of the true America, you who are killing my America."

"*Your* America, you Jew immigrant!" Quincy had grown furious.

"Jew immigrant, yes." David's eyes flashed and he held his head high. "But a Jew who knows that your Pilgrim fathers came straight out of his Old Testament, pure and consecrated of spirit, like Abraham led out of a land of oppression to seek a land of promise. It is you, freak fashionables seeking only your own selfish pleasures, blind and deaf to the meaning of America, using her only as a money bag to be squeezed for her dollars,—you who are undoing the work of Washington and Lincoln, vulgarizing your high heritage, and turning the last and noblest hope of humanity into a caricature."

"Ha! Ha! Ha! Ho! Ho! Ho!" laughed Quincy. "You never told me your Jew scribbler was a socialist."

"I am nothing but a simple artist." David's manner grew once more unassuming and boyish, but his tone thrilled through and through with the tensity of his earnestness. "But I came from

Europe one of her victims, and I know that she is a failure, that her palaces and peerages are outworn toys of the human spirit, and that the only hope of humanity lies in a new world. And here in the land of tomorrow, you are trying to bring back Europe."

"I wish we could," interjected Quincy.

"Europe with her comic opera coronets and her worm-eaten stage decorations and her pomp and chivalry built on a morass of crime and misery. But you shall not kill my dream. There shall come a fire round the crucible that will melt you—you and your breed—like wax in a blow pipe. America *shall* make good!" The restrained certainty of his quiet words cut like a knife.

Quincy was so angry that he clenched his fist and stood speechless.

At that Herr Pappelmeister, who had sat imperturbable throughout this remarkable scene, sprang up and began to wave his umbrella frantically.

"*Hoch* Quixano! Long live Quixano! *Hoch! Hoch!*" he cried.

"Poppy, you're dismissed," shouted Quincy and left the house at white heat. Mendel followed him hot on his heels in the vain hope of smoothing his ruffled feathers.

What on earth could his crazy David mean throwing such a chance away, thought Mendel.

"Oh, Herr Pappelmeister, you've lost your place!" said David.

"And saved my soul!" cried Pappelmeister. "Dollars are de devil. I blay me now good music and no more cheap stuff by command of Quincy Davenport!" And off he went, his very umbrella bristling with newly found self respect.

Vera and David were left alone. David feared lest Vera would leave him now in anger at what he had done, and never see him again, but Vera glowed with admiration at the courage of his stand. Vanished from her heart was all her old prejudice against the Jew, vanished from David's all instinct against the Gentile. And in that moment of uplifted feeling they both discovered they loved one another.

Later when Vera was gone and Mendel once more came home, David threw his arms boyishly around his uncle's neck.

"I am so happy, uncle," he said. "Vera will be my wife."

"Miss Revendal!" Mendel threw his nephew off as though he had struck him. "Have you lost your wits? Remember you are a Jew."

"Yes, and just think," said David, "she was bred up to despise Jews. Her father was a Russian baron."

"If she was the daughter of fifty barons, you could not marry her."

"Uncle," cried David in pained amaze. "You cling to old prejudice still? You who have come to the heart of the Crucible where the roaring fires of God are fusing our race with all the others."

"Not *our* race!" cried Mendel passionately. "Not your race and mine. The Jew has been tried in a thousand fires and only grown harder for them all."

"Fires of hate," answered David, "not fires of love. That is what melts. Here in this new republic we must look forward—"

"We must look backward too," interrupted Mendel.

"Backward—to what?" cried David. "To Kishineff and that butcher's face?"

"Hush!" Mendel was alarmed. "Calm yourself."

David struggled. "Yes, I will calm myself, but how else shall I do so, save by holding out my hands with prayer and music towards America, the Republic of Man and the Kingdom of God? The past I cannot mend. Take away the hope that I can mend the future and you make me mad."

"You are mad already—your dreams are mad. The Jew is hated here as elsewhere. You are false to your race."

"I keep faith with America. I have faith that America will keep faith with me."

"Go then," cried Mendel. "Marry your Gentile and be happy!"

"You turn me out?" asked David.

"You would not stay and break my mother's heart. You know she would mourn at your marrying a Gentile with the rending of garments and the seven days' sitting on the floor. Go! You have cast off the God of our Fathers."

"And the God of our *children!*" thundered David, "Does *He* demand no service?" But he had scarcely spoken so stormily when he grew suddenly quiet. Touching his uncle affectionately on the shoulder, he said slowly, "You are right, I must go."

"I'll hide the truth," said Mendel. "Mother must never know."

Just at that moment Frau Quixano was heard laughing uproariously with Kathleen in the kitchen.

"Ah!" said Mendel bitterly, "you've made this a merry Purim."

In rushed Frau Quixano with David's violin, begging him to play.

Mendel put out a protesting hand. "No, no, David, don't play now. I couldn't bear it."

"But I must," answered David. "You said she must never suspect, and it may be the last time I shall ever play for her." And he looked at the old woman lovingly as he took the fiddle and started the same old Slavic dance. Frau Quixano took a grotesque false nose from her pocket and clapped it on, laughing in childish glee. Torn between laughter and tears David laughed also.

"*Mutter!*" cried Mendel, shocked, but Frau Quixano's only answer to his dignified expostulation was to force a false nose on

him also, unwilling though he was, and she and Kathleen danced to David's music till they both fell breathless into a chair. Then with a sad and affectionate farewell glance at his grandmother David took his hat, his coat and his violin and slipped quietly out of the house that had sheltered him so long.

It was only a two dollar a month garret, six feet square, that he could afford henceforth, but then that was as large as a first class cabin on board a boat, so David had only to pretend he had a stateroom on the top deck of one of the great ocean liners, and it seemed quite luxurious and himself a millionaire at least! He and Vera were very happy though he was not earning nearly enough so they could even dream of marrying and setting up housekeeping yet.

When Quincy Davenport discovered that Vera had chosen to marry David, he made haste to send off at once to Europe for the Baron Revendal as the only means he could think of to prevent her wedding another. Now the Baron had never ceased to love and long for his daughter, and when he learned that she was on the point of marrying a Jew, he set out at once for America with his second wife, the Baroness, to try to prevent such an insult to the blood of the Revendals.

A tall, stern, grizzled man of military bearing was the Baron, with a narrow, fanatical forehead, yet of honest, even distinguished appearance. He had the nervous suspicious manner of a Russian official, who pays the penalty for his tyranny by constant terror of a revolutionist's bomb, and in self defence he always carried a pistol. The Baroness was a pretty but showy creature ablaze with barbaric jewels, and she was determined to have Vera marry Quincy for the sake of his heaps of good American dollars.

Ere the Baron had seen his daughter he regarded the Jews as the dirt beneath his feet and could talk of slaughtering Jews as impassively as of slaughtering swine.

"Shooting is too good for the enemies of Christ," he said to Quincy, devoutly crossing himself. "At Kishineff we stick the swine."

"Ah! I read about that. Did you see the massacre?" Quincy's attempt to appear unconcerned at this careless mention of such an atrocity was not altogether successful.

"Ah yes," answered the Baron. "I had charge of the whole district and I hurried a regiment up to teach the blaspheming brutes manners."

"My husband was decorated for it," said the Baroness, "he has the order of St. Vladimir."

And yet in Vera's hands when he found her once again after all their years of estrangement, the Baron was as wax.

"Christ save us!" he said at first when he heard her speak of her love for David. "You have become a Jewess."

"No more than David has become a Christian," answered Vera. "We were already at one. All honest people are. Surely, father, all religions must serve the same God since there is only one God to serve."

Never could the Baron forget that Vera was the same little motherless girl who had nestled against his breast in all her childish troubles and whom he had tenderly comforted. Almost before he knew it and in spite of the vehement expostulations of his wife, the Baron had promised Vera that he would see her young Jew whom she called such a talented musician, and Vera had great hopes that her father's love of music would melt all his prejudice when once he heard David play. The Baroness was incensed that her husband should even dream of agreeing to such a proposal and insisted on his taking her at once to her hotel since under no circumstances would she consent to be introduced to a Jew.

While the Baron was gone with the Baroness, Herr Pappelmeister turned up at the Settlement in search of David. Since he had left Quincy, Herr Pappelmeister had created an orchestra of his own and he came now to offer David a fine position as one of the first violins. It was joyous news to Vera, joyous news to David, for it meant that now at last they could really afford to marry.

"You're an angel, Herr Pappelmeister," cried Vera in delight.

"No, no, my dear child," laughed Pappelmeister, roguishly twirling himself round about to display his ample waist-line. "I fear dat I haf not de correct shape for an angel."

Nevertheless his goodness did not end even with his offer of the position to David. He had come furthermore to arrange with the young musician for the production of his symphony on the roof garden of the Settlement before all the immigrants there on the Fourth of July,—such a setting for his music as of all that were possible, David would most have desired.

"Played to the people! Under God's sky! On Independence Day! That will be perfect! It was always my dream to play it first to new immigrants, those who have known the pain of the old world and the hope of the new."

And when Herr Pappelmeister had left, David took up his fiddle and dashed into jubilant music.

"I will make my old fiddle strings burst with joy!" he cried.

"And nothing now shall part us!" cried Vera.

"Not all the Seven Seas could part you and me!" said David.

Just then came a knock at the door. They paid no heed, their happy faces showing no signs of hearing; then the door slightly opened and Baron Revendal looked hesitatingly in. As David perceived that face, his features worked convulsively, and the string of his violin broke with a tragic snap.

"The face! the face!" he muttered hoarsely and tottered backward into Vera's arms.

"David, what is it?" Vera steadied him in alarm.

"What is the matter with him?" harshly demanded the Baron.

David's violin and bow dropped from his grasp to the table.

"The voice!" he cried and struggling out of Vera's clasp he moved like one walking in his sleep toward the Baron. Putting out his hand, he testingly touched his face.

"Hands off!" the Baron shuddered at the mere touch of a Jew.

"A-ah!" David raised his voice in a mighty cry. "It is no vision! It is flesh and blood. No! it is stone, the man of stone. Monster!" And he raised one hand in a frenzy.

"Back, dog!" the Baron whipped out his pistol, but Vera with a shriek, darted in between the two.

Frozen again, David surveyed the pistol stonily. "Ho! You want my life too. Is the cry not yet loud enough?"

"The cry! What cry?" asked the Baron.

"The voice of the blood of my brothers crying out against you from the ground. Oh, how can you bear not to turn that pistol against yourself and execute upon yourself the justice which Russia denies you?"

"Tush!" said the Baron, shamefaced as he pocketed his pistol.

"Justice on himself!" cried Vera, "justice for what?"

"For crimes beyond human penalty!"

"David, you are raving. This is my father!"

"Your father!"—David staggered back as if struck in the face. "O God!"

The Baron tried to draw Vera toward him. "Come to me, Vera," he said.

"Don't touch me!" Vera shrank frantically away from his hand. "Say it is not true. It was the mob that massacred— *you* had no hand in it."

"I was there with my soldiers," the Baron answered sullenly.

"And you looked on with that cold face of hate!" hissed David, "while my mother—my sister—. Now and again you ordered your soldiers to fire!"

"Ah!" cried Vera in joyous relief. "Then he did check the mob. He did tell his soldiers to fire!"

"At any Jew who tried to defend himself!"

"Great God!" Vera fell on the sofa burying her face.

"It was the people avenging itself, Vera," the Baron explained.

"But you could have stopped them," she moaned.

"Who can stop a flood? I did my duty by Christ," he crossed himself, "and the Tsar."

"But you could have stopped them!"

"Silence!" The Baron's patience was gone. "You talk like an ignorant girl blinded by passion. Look up, little Vera." His voice grew suddenly tender. "You saw how papasha loves you, how he was ready to hold out his hand and how this cur tried to bite it! Be calm! Tell him a daughter of Russia cannot mate with dirt!"

"Father, I will be calm," Vera rose to her full height. "I was never absolutely sure of my love for him before—"

"Hah!" cried the Baron exultant, "she is a true Revendal!"

"But now—" she walked firmly toward the young Jew, "now David, I come to you and I say in the words of Ruth, thy people shall be my people and thy God my God."

"You shameless!" cried the Baron, but he stopped as he saw that David made no move to take Vera's outstretched hand.

"You cannot come to me," David's voice was low and icy. "There is a river of blood between us."

"Were it seven seas, love must cross them all," said Vera.

"Easy words to you. You never saw that red flood. Oh!" David covered his eyes with his hands while the Baron turned away in gloomy impotence. Then the young man sank into a chair and began to speak, quietly, almost dreamily.

"It was your Easter, and the air was full of holy bells and the streets of holy processions—priests in black and girls in white, waving palms and crucifixes, and everybody exchanging Easter eggs and kissing one another three times on the mouth in token of peace and good will, and even the Jew boy felt the spirit of love brooding over the earth. And what added to the peace and holy joy was that our own Passover was shining before us. My mother had already made the raisin wine, and my greedy little brother Solomon had sipped it on the sly that very morning. We were all at home—all except my father—he was away in the little synagogue where he was cantor. Ah! such a voice he had, and how we were looking forward to his hymns at the Passover table." David's voice broke for a moment and the Baron turned slowly toward him as if compelled against his will to listen to his story. "I was playing my cracked little fiddle. Little Miriam was making her doll dance to it. Ah, that decrepit old China doll, the only one the poor child had ever had—I can see it now— one eye, no nose, half an arm. We were all laughing to see it caper to my music. Suddenly my father flies in at the door, desperately clasping to his breast the Holy Scroll. We cry out to him to explain, and then we see that in that beloved mouth of song there is no longer a tongue! He tries to bar the door, a mob breaks in—we dash out through the back into the street. There are the soldiers—and the face—" Vera's eyes involuntarily sought the face of her father and he shrunk away from her glance. "When I came to myself, with a curious aching in my left shoulder, I saw lying beside me—Ah! by the crimson doll in the hand, I knew it must be little Miriam. The doll was a dream of perfection and beauty beside all that remained of my sister, my mother, of greedy little Solomon—" He broke down in ironic laughter.

"Hush, David," cried Vera. "Your laughter hurts more than tears. Let me comfort you."

But he pushed her forcibly from him. "For you I gave up my people. I darkened the home that sheltered me. There was always a still small voice calling me back, but I heeded nothing only the voice of the butcher's daughter. Let me go home—go home." And he turned unsteadily away. Perceiving how useless now was aught that could be said or done, Vera slipped like a shadow out of the room before him. To David the Baron cried suddenly, "Halt!" Whipping out his pistol once more, he advanced slowly toward the young man who stood still, expecting to be shot. But the Baron did not fire. He handed the pistol instead to David.

"You were right," he said, then he stepped back swiftly with a touch of stern heroism, in the attitude of a culprit at a military execution. "Shoot me."

David fingered the pistol and looked at it long and pensively as if with the sense of how little such a thing could accomplish in setting matters right. Then gradually his arm dropped and he let the pistol fall to the table. As he did so, his hand touched the string of his violin which yielded a little note. Thus reminded of his beloved fiddle, he picked it up and drew his fingers across the broken string.

"I must get a new string," he murmured and slowly dragged out of the room. "I must get a new string."

And so the Baron and Baroness were forced to go back to Russia without Vera, and Quincy was forced to give her up altogether. Vera kept on with her work at the Settlement though all the joy was gone out of it, and David went back to his people. But ah! for him, too, life was joyless after what he had done.

"You are stone all over, ever since you came back home," said Mendel. "Turned into a pillar of salt, Mother says, like Lot's wife!"

"That was the punishment for looking backward. Ah, uncle, there's more sense in that old Bible than the Rabbis suspect. Perhaps that is the secret of our people's suffering. We are always looking backward."

"I thought it was your Jewish heart that drove you back home to us, but if you are still hankering after Miss Revendal, I'd rather see you marry her than go about like this and so, I believe, would mother. You couldn't make the house any gloomier."

But in truth what troubled David most was the sense of his own defeat. He had preached of America as the great crucible wherein must be thrown all the old world hatreds to be melted by the fires of love, mutual forbearance, forgiveness and understanding, into a higher unity, and when the test had come home to him, when he had been asked to cast therein his long cherished and violent enmity, that it too might be purged away, he had refused. His own hatred, the hatred of Russian Jew for Russian Christian, deep grained though it had been and with good reason all down through the tragic years, was but a type of all the old world feuds that must here be yielded up to make the true American. And he had clung to his animosity, hugged it tight. He who had talked always of looking away from the past and the God of our fathers toward the future and the God of our children, when the test had come to him, had clung to the past and let it ruin the future. He had pushed away from him one whom he loved and who loved him because he still clung to his hatreds, his hatreds and the past. Ah, he knew he was false, false to his vision, false to America, false to his music.

So came the evening of the eventful Fourth of July. At the Settlement House it seemed that David's life-long ambition had been fulfilled at last. His symphony was played by Herr Pappelmeister's orchestra before all that crowd of wanderers from the old world, and they had understood his music with their hearts and souls, and applauded and applauded, and cried out again and again for the composer to show himself before them. It seemed a remarkable triumph. Yet up on the roof garden of the Settlement House, refusing to come down and take to himself the plaudits, sat David all alone. From the depths of his soul he knew it had not been a triumph.

The sun was setting and below him stretched out a beautiful far-reaching panorama of New York. Irregular rose the sky line of that mighty city and off to the right lay the harbor with its gilded Statue of Liberty. Everything was wet and gleaming, for the sun had come out after rain. In the sky hung heavy clouds through which thin golden lines of sunset were just beginning to labor. David, hugging tight his violin case, sat on a bench and gazed moodily at the sky, while the enormous sounds of applause, muffled by the distance, rose up to him from below. Thither came Mendel and Herr Pappelmeister to congratulate him on his success. They roused no joy in his soul. He knew he had been a failure. Thither came Kathleen and Frau Quixano, also, on the same errand bent. It was Shabbos and Frau Quixano had climbed wearily puffing and panting up flight after flight of stairs rather than use the elevator and fail to keep her Shabbos. And lo! Kathleen, late bitter foe of all things Jewish, was escorting the old lady in her slow tottering course toward David with the air of a guardian angel, and lo! the old lady herself, lately cursing all things American, was wearing a tiny American flag in honor of the day. Ah! that was what David's America did to all races who came to her shore, each one giving to and accepting from the others, each melting into the whole, transforming and being transformed, till at last shall come the real American to embody all the best in the world.

"When you take your mistress down again, Kathleen, please don't let her walk," said David sweetly, after the old lady had satisfied herself by laughing and crying over him.

"But Shabbos isn't out yet!"

David smiled, "There's no harm, Kathleen, in going *down* in the elevator."

"Troth, I'll egshplain to her that droppin' down isn't ridin'," chuckled Kathleen.

"Tell her dropping down is natural not *work* like flying up."

But when Kathleen turned to look for Frau Quixano, she had wandered off over the rooftop in the wrong direction entirely.

"*Wu geht Ihr, bedad?*" Kathleen called after her in a ridiculous mixture of Irish and Yiddish. "*Houly Moses, komm' zurick!*" And as she took Frau Quixano by the arm and led her carefully off toward the elevator, she added over her shoulder, *"Begorra!* we Jews never know our way!"

Scarcely had David been left alone, when Vera came to the rooftop to convey to him from Miss Andrews the heartfelt thanks and congratulations of the Settlement. It was two months since they had seen each other.

"Please don't *you* congratulate me too," said David. "That would be too ironical. How can I endure all these congratulations when I know what a terrible failure I have made?"

"Failure!" cried Vera. "You have produced something real and new, a most wonderful success."

"Failure! Failure!" cried David. "Every bar of my music cried, 'Failure'. It shrieked from the violins, blared from the trombones, thundered from the drums. It was written on all the faces—"

"Oh no! no!" Vera spoke vehemently. "I watched the faces, those faces of toil and sorrow, those faces from many lands. They were fired by your vision of their coming brotherhood, lulled by your dream of their land of rest. And I could see you were right in speaking to the people. In some strange beautiful way the inner meaning of your music stole into all those simple souls—"

"And my soul, my soul!" cried David springing up. "What of my soul? False to its own music, its own mission, its own dream. That is what I mean by failure, Vera. I preached of God's crucible, this great new continent that could melt up all race differences and vendettas, that could purge and re-create and make anew. And God tried me with his supremest test. He gave me a heritage from the old world, hate and vengeance and blood, and said, 'Cast it all into my crucible.' And I said, 'Even thy crucible cannot melt this hate!' And so I sat crooning over the dead past, gloating over the old blood-stains, I, the apostle of America, the prophet of the God of our children. Oh, how my music mocked me! And you, so fearless, so high above all that has come to pass, how you must despise me, despise me!"

"I?" cried Vera. "Ah no!"

"You must! You do. Your words still sting. 'Were it seven seas between us,' you said, 'love must cross them.' And I—I who had prated of seven seas—"

"Not seas of blood," cried Vera. "I spoke selfishly, thoughtlessly. I had not realized what that sea had meant for you. Now I see it day and night."

"There lies my failure," said David. "To have brought it to your eyes instead of blotting it from my own."

"No man could have blotted it out." Vera shuddered.

"Yes," cried David, "by faith in the crucible. But in the supreme moment, my faith was found wanting. You came to me and I thrust you away. Ah! you can never forgive me."

"Forgive!" cried Vera. "It is I that should go down on my knees to you for my father's sin."

"No," David's voice rang strong with conviction. "The sins of the fathers shall *not* be visited upon the children. You owe me nothing." He suddenly stretched out both hands. "Come to me, Vera! Cling to me!"

"Shall I come to you and let the shadows of Kishineff hang over all your years to come?"

"Yes." He took both her hands in a firm, strong clasp as though he would never again let her go. "Cling to me despite it all, cling to me till all those ugly memories vanish, cling to me till love shall triumph over death."

"I dare not," Vera drew back. "It will make you remember."

"It will make me forget."

There was a pause of hesitation, then Vera said very slowly:

"I yield. I will kiss you as we Russians kiss at Easter, the three kisses of peace." And she kissed him solemnly three times on the mouth as in a ritual ceremony.

"See," said David calmly. "Easter was the date of the massacre, yet now when you speak of it I am disturbed no more."

IN SHINING ARMOR

Vera spoke fervently. "God grant that peace may endure."

For a moment they stood hand in hand by the parapet over-looking the mighty city below, then Vera said softly, "Look how beautiful is the sunset after the storm." The sunset had indeed reached its most magnificent moment. Above the golden saffron that lay along the horizon, the whole sky was burning flame.

"It is the fires of God round his crucible," said David pointing downward. "There she lies, the great melting pot. Listen— can't you hear the roaring and the bubbling? There gapes her mouth,—" he pointed toward the east— "the harbor where a thousand mammoth feeders come from the ends of the world to pour in their human freight. Ah, what a stirring and a seeth-ing! Celt and Latin, Slav and Teuton, Greek and Syrian—"

"Jew and Gentile," added Vera drawing closer to him.

"Yes, east and west, and north and south—how the great Alchemist melts and fuses them with his purging flame! Here shall they all unite to build the Republic of Man and the Kingdom of God. Ah, Vera, what is the glory of Rome and Jerusalem where all nations and races come to worship and look back com-pared to the glory of America where all races and nations come to *labor* and *look forward?*"

There was an instant's solemn pause. The sunset faded swiftly and the whole vast panorama below was suffused with a restful twilight, while the lights of the town, gleaming out through the dusk, added to all the tender scene, the poetry of the night. Far back over the darkening water, like a lonely guiding star, twinkled the torch of the Statue of Liberty. From below some-where came the sound of voices singing the national anthem:

"*My country, 'tis of thee,*
Sweet land of Liberty
Of thee I sing."

David stood with Vera close by his side, his heart purified

David's aim to get this New World, with its new rhythms and life into music, was attained by the Bohemian composer, Dvorak, in his *New World Symphony*, begun in a picturesque settlement of Bohemians at Spillville, Iowa.

at last of the hideous stains of the past, his shining face turned transfigured toward the future alone, the future with all its glorious possibilities of working for the fulfillment of his dream, for the revelation in the hearts of men of that true America of liberty, humanity, brotherhood and justice. Slowly he raised his hands as in benediction over the shining city below.

"Peace, peace," he said, "to all ye unborn millions, fated to fill this giant continent. The God of our *children* give you peace."

YOUR AMERICA

An Address to New-Made Citizens

By Woodrow Wilson

YOU have just taken an oath of allegiance to the United States. Of allegiance to whom? Of allegiance to no one, unless it be to God.

You have taken an oath of allegiance to a great ideal, to a great body of principles, to a great hope of the human race. You have said, "We are going to America not only to earn a living, not only to seek the things which it was more difficult to obtain where we were born, but to help forward the great enterprises of the human spirit—to let men know that everywhere in the world there are men who will cross strange oceans and go where a speech is spoken which is alien to them, knowing that whatever the speech, **there is but one longing and utterance of the human heart, and that is for liberty and justice."**

Through his tragic acquaintance with the poor in the ghettos and slums of Europe, Israel Zangwill, a Jewish novelist of England, saw America, the New World, as the great hope for the oppressed of the Old World. Woodrow Wilson, in his address to these new-made citizens tried to impress them with the duty they had as Americans to uphold and work for this great ideal—the American Dream of a richer life for all.